Maggie Adams, Dancer

Maggie Adams, Dancer

A Novel by Karen Strickler Dean

Chapter Illustration by Phyllis Herfield

AN AVON CAMELOT BOOK

MAGGIE ADAMS, DANCER is an original publication of
Avon Books.
This work has never before appeared in book form.

AVON BOOKS
A division of
The Hearst Corporation
959 Eighth Avenue
New York, New York 10019

First Camelot Printing, April, 1980

CAMELOT TRADEMARK REG. U.S. PAT. OFF. AND IN
OTHER COUNTRIES, MARCA REGISTRADA, HECHO EN
U.S.A.

Printed in the U.S.A.

10 9 8 7 6 5 4 3 2

Dedicated to the memory of
Francesca Romanoff

Chapter One

All my life I have heard Cinderella stories about a nobody stepping at a moment's notice into a starring role. I never dreamed it would happen to me, though, a real nobody—a mere fourteen-year-old ballet student with frizzy red hair and braces on my teeth.

But now, two weeks before Christmas, on the night of our charity dress rehearsal, it actually was happening to me.

It started with someone banging on the door of the dressing room I shared with my best friends, Lupe and Joyce.

"Maggie! I'm coming in!" yelled a frantic voice I recognized as belonging to Ian McMichael, our company director, ballet teacher, and former principal dancer with American Ballet.

My friends and I looked at each other and shrugged. We had already warmed our muscles, put on our makeup, and changed out of the party dresses we wore in the first act ball scene. We were waiting for the second act of the *Nutcracker Ballet* to begin.

Our dressing room door rattled and shuddered. I expected McMichael's fist to splinter the thin plywood.

"Well, come on in!" my friend Joyce finally shouted.

The door flew open and in plunged McMichael, hugging a mass of pink satin and net.

"Here, Maggie. Get into this. You've got to dance Sugarplum."

He shoved the costume at me. He set a thin silver tiara on the dressing table. I clutched the costume. I crossed my fingers. It was happening! It really was happening to me! And the starring role I, a nobody, was stepping into at a moment's notice, was Sugarplum Fairy. It's a part I've dreamed of dancing ever since Mama took me to see *Nutcracker* when I was four years old.

Suddenly, a thought hit me like a fist in the stomach.

"But I can't remember the steps," I cried.

McMichael blinked his bloodshot eyes and scrubbed one hand through his thinning gray hair.

"Nonsense! Of course you remember them, my dear. You practiced the steps behind Martina when she came down from the City."

I uncrossed my fingers and pushed at a frizz of my red hair that was escaping from its net.

"She only came down a few times. I wasn't really her understudy, you know. And that Larry Randall wouldn't even practice the lifts with me."

McMichael continued to rub his head.

"I know Randall is difficult. Very difficult. But you

8

know all the lifts. I taught them to you in partnering class."

"That's not the same," I said. "I've never done them with him."

McMichael started toward the door.

"You'll remember the steps, Maggie. And you'll do the lifts just fine."

I fluttered after McMichael.

"And my blister, the one on my right big toe. It's gotten worse since yesterday."

I tapped the end of my right toe shoe on the floor and shuddered with the pain.

"See? It kills me to go *en pointe*."

McMichael did not look back.

"Relax, Maggie. Don't worry about yourself. You can do it!"

I stared at McMichael's slight, straight shoulders. Maybe I could. If he thought so. I wanted to, so much. More than anything in the world I wanted to be a really good dancer.

McMichael opened the door to leave.

"What's happened to Martina?" I asked, suddenly wondering why I was stepping at a moment's notice into her starring role.

McMichael's eyes rolled ceiling-ward.

"Tendonitis, the doctor thinks. Martina's got it in her left knee."

"But she was okay in company class this afternoon," I said.

He nodded.

"She was all right an hour ago, too. Or if she wasn't, she didn't say anything."

My stomach still fluttered, but I felt suddenly glad that the City was fifty miles away.

"So it's too late to get another dancer from the City, isn't it?" I said.

"Yes. If she'd only said something even an hour ago. But—no! Fortunately, tonight is only the charity dress rehearsal. We'll be able to get another principal down for the weekend performances."

McMichael started through the door again, but Joyce blocked his way with the great hooped skirts of her Mother Ginger costume. She jutted her strong chin.

"Listen, Mr. McMichael. Maggie dances better than any of those City Ballet soloists. Or even the principals. She should dance Sugarplum this weekend, too."

I pushed at the hair escaping from the coil at the nape of my neck and waited for McMichael to explode. To my surprise, he didn't. He merely raised his eyebrows, scrubbed at his hair, and with his foot nudged aside Joyce's huge skirt.

"A slight exaggeration, my dear. And kindly get that skirt out of my way. Maggie dances very well, but she's only a student. That's good enough for a charity performance, but people will pay good money to see City Ballet principals. Which they won't to watch a fourteen-year-old ballet student."

McMichael plunged out the door and then paused.

"Besides, there are those braces on your teeth, Maggie. I think they're what Randall objects to most."

I clapped my hand over my mouth.

"Randall's a big jerk!" Joyce said, slamming the door closed.

My friend Lupe put her arms around me. She was small and had skin the color of cinnamon. Through the white nightgown she wore as Clara in the second

10

act, I felt how thin she had grown lately. She kissed both my cheeks.

"Please don't cry, *cariña*. You're better than any of those principals. Except maybe Martina."

I hugged Lupe, but couldn't stop crying. Also, my blister stung.

"You're sweet, Lupe. But Randall's right. These awful braces!"

"Stop worrying about them, Mag," Joyce said. "Nobody notices them except you—and that creepy Randall!"

"What Joyce says is true," Lupe said. "People see only that you dance like an angel."

I wiped at my eyes, careful not to smear my makeup.

"Thanks, but even my orthodontist says I'm the original flash-in-the-pan dancer."

"You'll get your braces off soon," Lupe said, patting me.

A knock shook the plywood door again. It was McMichael once more.

"Get into that costume, Maggie. And get up those stairs."

Lupe helped me out of my costume for the Rose, the role I was supposed to dance. Joyce handed me McMichael's pink mass of satin and net. Lupe reached up and smoothed my hair. Joyce fastened the little silver tiara to the crown of my head.

I stared at myself in the mirror.

"At least the tiara matches my braces," I said, starting to cry again.

"Relax," Joyce said. "You look great. The costume even fits. Which is a miracle. Lord knows where McMichael dug it up."

The tutu did flare crisply at my hips and the bodice

11

fit snugly. Except at the top. A problem Joyce solved by snatching several tissues from the box on the dressing table. She tucked them into the little darted cups which I was too flat to fill.

"*Violà!*" she said. "Here we have a ballerina as elegant as any from the City Ballet."

When the mirror told me she was right, the steps I thought I had forgotten came gliding back. My blister stopped stinging.

Lupe hugged me.

"You'll do fine, *cariña.*"

I nodded. But to make really sure, I crossed my fingers before clattering with my friends up the stairs to dance the role of the Sugarplum Fairy—at a moment's notice

Chapter Two

When my friends and I reached the wings, the first person we saw was Larry Randall, who was suddenly to be my partner in the *Nutcracker*.

Only we had never practiced together. How would he balance me in the supported turns? Did I dare ask him to do a few lifts with me before the second act curtain? I did not!

Look at him there under the working lights. His blond hair, which he must plaster down with brilliantine, gleamed like glossy yellow kitchen paint. His long, well-shaped nose and strong chin gave him a movie actor's profile, but when he turned full face I only noticed how cold his milky blue eyes seemed. His thin nostrils, which flared when he was angry, were flaring now.

Joyce pushed me toward him.

"You've got to know how he'll hold you in the turns. Ask him to practice with you."

I shook my head.

"I couldn't. He's already angry. He's probably heard he has to partner me."

"Come on, Mag," Joyce said. "Don't be stupid. Lupe and I'll go with you, won't we, Lupe?"

Lupe opened her dark eyes wider and backed away.

"*Por dios*, no! I've got to be ready for my first entrance."

She ducked into the crowd of dancers, but Joyce dragged me toward Randall. When we were close to him, she gave me another shove.

"Go on. Tell him."

I crossed my fingers.

"Mr. Randall—"

"Louder," Joyce whispered. "You'll have to shout because the crowd out front is getting so noisy."

I bit my lip and then said his name again.

This time he turned to look at me. I no longer saw his handsome profile, only a mask of heavy pink makeup through which his blue-outlined eyes froze me.

"Are you addressing me, young lady?"

"I—I—I'm Maggie Adams. And you're supposed to partner me tonight."

He arched one penciled eyebrow and glanced toward the clock above the panel of levers used to control the lighting.

"So?"

I tried to back away, but Joyce blocked my escape with her Mother Ginger skirts. Finally, words came tumbling out.

"I'm wondering if we could practice a few lifts together since we never have."

His blue-lined eyelids dropped over his eyes.

14

"And never shall," he said, turning his back on me and striding away.

My face stung as if he had slapped it. Joyce swung herself and her skirts alongside of me.

"Never shall, *indeed!* What does he mean by that? And for heaven's sake, don't cry, Mag. You'll ruin your makeup. Come on. We're going after him."

She pushed through the crowd of dancers and stagehands and around giant green prop boxes and pieces of scenery. In front of us, like a bright balloon, floated Randall's blond head. I tried to break away from Joyce.

"It won't do any good. You heard him."

Joyce swayed on in her wide skirts, dragging me with her. We caught up with him in front of the lighting panel. He looked at the clock again. Joyce pushed me toward him, but I hung back. She lifted her chin.

"Well, then, *I'll* have a try."

Joyce is seventeen and, because her mother is divorced and works, she has taken care of herself for a long time. Maybe that's why she has a lot more courage than I have.

"Mr. Randall, if you don't practice some lifts with Maggie, you're both likely to fall flat on your faces."

Randall gave her his cold blue glance. His nostrils flared.

"Not that it's any of your business, dear young lady, but I don't plan to do any lifts with her—ever!"

Even Joyce's firm chin sagged, but she soon raised it again.

"How can you avoid it? She's dancing Sugarplum tonight."

His face remained expressionless under the pink makeup.

15

"That's extremely unlikely. But even if she does, I'm not dancing with her. I'm marking."

"You're kidding!" was all Joyce was able to say.

His painted lips parted in a smile, if you could call it that.

"No, I'm not 'kidding,' as you put it. I always mark rehearsals. I just walk through the part, do enough to establish my positions on stage and let the conductor set the timing on me."

For a minute I forgot my fear. I believe that if you're going to dance, you should dance full-out.

"This is not a rehearsal!" I cried. "It's a performance for all those people out there who can't afford to buy tickets for the weekend."

Joyce's jaw tightened.

"Even if you don't care about the audience, how about our little regional company and the kids from the ballet school? All of us are knocking ourselves out to put on a good *Nutcracker*."

I nodded and pointed out Lupe standing *en pointe* in one of the shallow boxes of crushed rosin.

"See that little girl in the white nightgown? That's Lupe, and she's dancing the role of Clara. She's barely thirteen and is as excited as if she really were Clara, traveling through a magic candyland."

Joyce hardly let me finish.

"How do you think she'll feel about the big star from City Ballet, marking? If you won't dance for the audience, dance for Lupe and the rest of the kids. They're the future dancers of this country."

Randall laughed in our faces.

"Don't delude yourselves. Not a single member of this little company..."

He paused disdainfully in mid-sentence.

"By the way, just what is it called, this little group of amateurs?"

I stared at him. He didn't even know the name of the company that was paying him. Or pretended he didn't.

"It's called the Santa Inez Regional Ballet Company," I said stiffly. "And belongs to the National Association."

He gave me a mock bow.

"Thank you very much. As I was saying, not a single member of this company shows enough talent to become a professional dancer! Including the two of you. Now stop bothering me."

We watched him saunter away.

"Jerk!" Joyce said. "He's probably right about me, but I doubt that he's ever looked far enough beyond his simply divine profile to notice your perfect body type or your dancing. Or Lupe's either."

I pushed at my chignon.

"I don't know," I said. "I just know I've got to be a dancer."

Joyce patted my shoulder.

"And you will be, Mag. You are a dancer. Tonight you're dancing Sugarplum."

She thumbed her nose at departing Randall.

"And if he wants to mark, let him. It'll make you look all the better."

I sighed.

"I hope you're right. Do you really think he means to mark?"

"You heard him."

"Then we should warn McMichael."

Joyce shook her head.

"I'm sure he knows already."

I stared after Randall's yellow head.

"Well, I'm dancing full-out. And if he doesn't do the lifts with me, I'll improvise."

At that moment I saw McMichael come out of

Martina's dressing room. Randall hurried up to him. Both of them looked at the clock. Randall flared his nostrils and McMichael scrubbed at his head.

"Now poor old McMichael's getting it from Randall. I wonder why McMichael doesn't boot him out of the way and start the second act? The audience sounds ready to tear the place apart."

The roar of the crowd was almost, but not quite, loud enough now to drown out the tuning-up trills and scales of the high school orchestra.

I was just able to make out the xylophone singing the Sugarplum theme. My music. I crossed my fingers. For the first time tonight, I really believed I would dance Sugarplum.

Inside my chest stirred my summer wind—a special happiness I get when I dance. What did it matter if Randall marked or didn't mark? In moments, I would dance Sugarplum.

Chapter Three

I was still listening to the Sugarplum theme when I felt a rush of cold air on my back. Behind me, McMichael said, "Finally!"

Turning around, I saw him lead through the stage door a slender young woman wrapped in a trench coat. From the crown of her head swung a thick brown ponytail. From one shoulder bumped a large leather case. She carried a pink costume shrouded in a plastic bag.

I stared. I froze and burned as if I were packed in dry ice.

Here came the reason for the delay in starting the second act. All along, McMichael had been preparing me only as an understudy in case Linda Larson failed to arrive in time to dance Sugarplum tonight.

I backed against the cold plaster wall and tried not to watch McMichael go past with Linda Larson. But

I couldn't help noticing that he never glanced at me, his favorite pupil for the past five years.

Joyce stood as close to me as the wide skirts of her costume allowed.

"Treachery! Pure treachery!" she said.

McMichael must have heard her because he began rubbing his head.

Linda Larson was smiling, of course. It was easy to see that she liked being treated as if she were Makarova, my favorite ballerina, instead of a thin little soloist guesting with a regional company. But I'd have given anything to be Linda Larson tonight and dance Sugarplum.

"She doesn't have time to warm up and make up!" Joyce said, beside me.

"That's not my problem," I said, pushing past Joyce's skirts. "I'm getting out of here."

I dodged through the crowd of dancers and headed toward the stairway.

At least my parents and Doug, who had come to see me perform the Rose variation, didn't know I had almost danced Sugarplum. Mama hoped I'd be lovely as the Rose. My father hoped I'd blow it and decide to become something practical like a secretary, or a computer programmer, or a doctor like he was. And Doug? I didn't know what Doug hoped.

At the top of the stairs, Joyce grabbed me by the shoulder. Her skirts swung against my legs.

"Don't do anything stupid, Mag. You're still dancing Rose. Next to Sugarplum that's the best role in *Nutcracker*."

I turned away.

"It's not the same."

"Don't be childish, Mag. Get back into your Rose costume. We need you."

My toe shoes chattering on the concrete, I ran

down the stairs. My blister stung. Because of her skirts, Joyce could not keep up with me.

I ran into the dressing room and locked the door. For a moment I stared at myself in the pink costume. My red hair frizzed out of the net. Gray tears snailed down my cheeks leaving trails of eyeliner. My braces seemed to sneer at me.

Flinging myself away from the mirror, I tore off the Sugarplum costume and pulled on my jeans and sweater.

A gentle knock sounded on the door. Who was there? It couldn't be Joyce. The knock was too timid. And certainly not McMichael. Lupe, maybe, come to comfort me with her soft Spanish endearments and one of her hugs. But I didn't want to see even thin little Lupe.

The knock came again.

"Maggie, I want to talk to you. I want to explain what happened."

It was McMichael. I pressed my hands to my ears. I didn't answer. I wouldn't listen.

"Maggie, I'm sorry. I really am, but it had to be this way. Randall threatened to quit all the *Nutcracker* performances unless we got a replacement from City Ballet tonight. So we called Linda Larson. She lives only twenty miles from here."

Inside the door, I wrapped my arms across my chest. I rocked myself. I cried. McMichael's feet shuffled around on the concrete floor of the corridor.

"Of course Linda won't have time to make-up or warm up," he continued. "She'll have to mark. But Randall insists on marking anyway."

He paused. Now he would tell me to get back in the Rose costume. I was to dance the Rose variation, after all.

Well, I wouldn't get back in that old red satin thing

21

tonight! It could stay right on that rack where Lupe hung it when she helped me change. But where was it? Only our first act party dresses hung on the rack.

Outside the door McMichael continued to shuffle.

"And Maggie, there's something else. When I asked you to dance Sugarplum, I had to get somebody to dance the Rose. So I asked Cynthia Bellermont."

I flung myself onto a stool. So that's where the Rose costume was. On fat Cynthia! Ida, our wardrobe mistress, must have worked an instant miracle ripping out darts and tearing out seams to widen the bodice enough for Cynthia!

"Right now," McMichael continued, "Mrs. Bellermont's waiting with her daughter in the wings. So I'll have to let Cynthia dance Rose. You know Mrs. Bellermont!"

I did, indeed!

Besides being the pushiest kind of ballet mother, Mrs. Bellermont was the pushy president of the Ballet Auxiliary. She spent all her time, and I'll bet half her money, trying to persuade McMichael to put Cynthia in my roles. And Mrs. Bellermont would probably force McMichael to keep her daughter in my role all this weekend.

A minute ago nobody could have forced me to dance the Rose. But I certainly didn't want Cynthia ruining it!

"She'll wobble every turn and jerk all the jumps!" I cried.

"Let's hope she won't, Maggie."

"You know she will!"

"Sometimes we have to compromise a little. I know you could dance Sugarplum beautifully, but you're only a student. You should be dancing the Rose, but you'll dance it this weekend. I promise."

I shook my head so violently that my hair flapped around my face. This weekend, he said. But what about my parents, and Doug, and all the others out there? What would they think when Cynthia ruined my Rose variation and the principals marked? Well, I wouldn't wait around to find out. I'd leave. I'd leave right now.

Out in the corridor McMichael cleared his throat.

"And one more thing, Maggie. You're to come upstairs and watch from the wings. I want you to see any changes we make."

I flounced off the stool. This was too much!

"Mr. McMichael, I don't intend to watch Cynthia and your great artists from City Ballet goof up *Nutcracker*."

"Don't behave like a brat," McMichael said sharply. "Remember you're a member of the company. You take the downs with the ups. Report to the wings immediately!"

I obeyed.

I don't remember going up the stairs, but I do remember the stage manager calling, "Places, please. Places." From the other side of the stage the colored gels on the pole lights glared into my eyes.

Around me huddled groups of children pretending to be Spanish dancers or candy canes or gingerbread boys. And every once in a while I saw Lupe blotting away sweat with a Kleenex and crossing herself before her next entrance.

When I heard the orchestra begin the "Waltz of the Flowers," I spotted fat Cynthia in my let-out crimson tutu. Clumping through the middle of the group of waltzing flowers, she stumbled off every pirouette and jerked all the *grands jetés*. It's a wonder she didn't snap that thick, white neck of hers!

Finally, Sugarplum's music began. Earlier, when

the orchestra was tuning up, this melody stirred in me the lovely feeling I call my summer wind. But now the music wasn't mine. I shut my eyes so that I wouldn't see Linda Larson and Larry Randall mark their roles.

When the final curtain struck the floor, I dashed down to the dressing room, stuffed my soggy toe shoes and damp tights into my ballet bag, and rushed out of the theatre.

Chapter Four

Outside, a cold wind skidded around the corners of the theatre. On the standards of the street lamps, Christmas decorations swung and creaked.

I took a deep breath and buttoned my coat. I tied a scarf over my head to warm my ears and to keep my hair from lashing my face. How glad I was to leave the stuffy theatre!

I ran down the steps and across to the parking lot. I looked at the rows and rows of cars. Where was my parents' car? Or Doug's? But even if I found one or both, how could I get in?

I had no keys to unlock the doors.

And, anyway, did I really want to creep in and wait for Doug? Or my parents? Tonight I could do without Mama's hug.

"There'll be other times, Maggie!"

Or my father's sarcasm.

"Aren't you supposed to be the best in the

company? Maybe they're saving you for more important occasions!"

Doug might pass it off casually, mutter, "Tough luck, Mag!" But I did not want anyone to say anything.

I hugged my coat against the wind and hoisted my ballet bag higher on my shoulder. I would walk the five miles home, starting here at the new civic center, where the lights of our pretty wedding-cake-of-a-theatre flamed into the night.

First, I had to hurry through what remained of dark, narrow, old town after the urban renewal program gave us the civic center. Soon, though, I would come to the ample streets of the suburbs where houses, mostly rambling and one-storied, and nests of shopping centers now paved most of the valley. When my parents first moved here, they said fields and orchards spread from one rounded coastal range to the other.

With the wind pushing at my back, I left the parking lot and rushed along the sidewalk into the old part of town. Maybe this walk in the cold would help me forget Randall and the *Nutcracker*.

A car or two passed me. I noticed one edging along the curb beside me. Following me? A horn tooted. I stared hard at the vacant store fronts. Windows painted white turned into blind eyes. Against my feet fluttered a crumpled newspaper. A crushed styro-foam cup cartwheeled past and an empty beer can clattered along the gutter.

The car continued to roll along the curb. Fear touched deep inside me. This midnight walk was not such a good idea after all. I turned and ran back toward the theatre. Headlights were flashing on in the parking lot. If I could reach it, I would be safe.

Behind me, someone yelled.

"Mag, for crying out loud!"

Doug! It was Doug!

Warm with relief, I turned around. He was coming after me on foot. His family's car stood at the curb where he had left it.

I waited for him. Tall and lanky, he came toward me, his hands in the pockets of his overcoat. His head was bare, but his blond hair was too short and too curly for the wind to bother.

"Mag, what got into you?"

"Nothing."

Now that I recognized Doug, I felt silly. And annoyed.

"Nothing got into me. Can't a person take a walk without being followed? You scared me."

"For gosh sakes, Mag. I saw you leave the parking lot. Didn't you recognize my car?"

"I never notice what cars look like. I just saw a car following me and got scared."

"Sorry, Mag."

He put out a hand to touch my arm, but I dodged out of his reach. He made a second try and grabbed my arm.

"Come on, Mag. What kind of craziness is this? Get in the car. I'll take you home."

I tried to free my arm, but he held on.

"Let go," I said. "I told you, I'm walking home."

"But, Mag, it's midnight and cold. And you live way out in the suburbs. Too far to walk. Besides this part of town's no place for you!"

"I don't care," I said. And I didn't. I wanted to walk and walk.

"Are you acting like this because you didn't get to dance tonight? It's not a matter of life or death."

27

I looked at him. He didn't understand anything!

"Well, to me it is. Anyway, I don't want to talk about it."

"Okay, we won't talk about it, but get in the car before this wind freezes us to death."

I shivered.

"All right, but I want to go straight home. And I don't want to talk."

"Suits me."

I opened the car door, and he went around to the driver's side.

"I don't know if it's better when you are dancing or when you aren't," he said, sliding into the car.

I stared across the narrow dirty sidewalk at a blank store front.

"I told you I didn't want to talk."

He started the car and pulled away from the curb.

"When you aren't dancing, you're impossible," he said as if he hadn't heard me. "And when you are, you have no time for me."

I faced him.

"And what about basketball? I suppose that doesn't take any time."

"It's an after-school sport, Mag. Not my whole life. Not like your ballet. Answer me this—except at school, how many times have I seen you since August?"

I shrugged. He sounded annoyed.

"You do remember that we met last August, don't you?"

"Of course, I do!"

Why was I being so nasty when I did remember that wonderful hot August morning at Stevenson High's freshman orientation? A junior, he volunteered to show around some of us freshmen.

28

I remembered him at the head of our group. Tall, gangly, almost six-feet-four. His blond curls reminded me of the picture of the god Apollo in my social studies book.

That morning he caught me staring but didn't look away. He smiled a wide friendly smile not spoiled by braces. His Adam's apple bounced like a tennis ball up and down his strong throat.

After the tour he twisted his hands behind him and asked, "How about a Coke?"

But that was a hot August morning and this was a cold December midnight. I slid deeper into my coat and stared out the windshield.

"Except at school," he said, "I haven't seen you more than four times. It seems like you always have a ballet class or a rehearsal or a performance. When are you going to get this out of your system?"

I pulled my coat around me. He sounded like my father, the doctor, in more ways than one.

"It's not a disease!" I said. "Dancing's the most important thing in my life."

"You're telling me. How do you think that makes me feel?"

I looked at the soft outline of his curly head against the lighted window of a house we passed as we drove into the suburbs. If he felt jealous of my dancing, he must like me. I liked Doug too, but I couldn't give up ballet.

Pretty soon he stopped in front of my house. It was dark except for the light we always left on in Mama's dressing room and the amber lamps that bloomed like flowers on wrought-iron stems along the driveway. My parents were not home from the theatre yet.

For a moment we sat without speaking. Outside,

the wind battered the windows and fenders, swept a handful of dry leaves from our huge old oak tree across the hood. I heard the leather seat sigh when Doug slid toward me. I reached for the door handle.

"I have to go in," I said, pushing down on the handle. The door didn't open.

"This door's stupid!"

"It's not the door that's stupid!" Doug snapped.

"Are you saying that I'm stupid?"

Doug sighed.

"I'm not saying anything, Mag. I like you. And if ballet didn't take all your time, we could really have fun together."

I sighed, too. I leaned back against the seat.

"I have to dance."

"All the time?"

"You can't dance part-time. If you want to be a dancer, you have to dance hours and hours every day."

He shrugged.

"But can't we be friends?"

He slid along the front seat and put his arm around me. I tugged at the door handle again.

"I have to go in, Doug. My parents will be back any minute."

"Come on, Mag, let me kiss you goodnight. You never have."

His voice sounded soft. I wanted his arms around me. I wanted him to kiss me, but how do you kiss somebody with braces on your teeth?

My parents' car drove up. The headlights splashed an icy whiteness through Doug's car.

"Please open the door for me."

"Yeah. Sure."

He reached across in front of me.

"You pull up. Up! Why can't you remember that?"

The door swung open and I got out. I held onto it for a minute. I didn't want him to go away mad at me.

"Well, thanks for the ride, Doug."

"Yeah. Sure. Shut the door, will you? See you around sometime."

I stood in the wind, watching his car move off down the dark street. When his taillights disappeared around the corner, I ducked under the dark mass of our oak tree and up the slope of lawn. Tonight was sure not my night!

3

Chapter Five

The wind followed me up the front steps and clanged the lid of the wrought-iron mailbox. In the distance, I heard Doug's car squawk around a corner.

I also heard our garage door slam open against the rafters. That meant my father was still outside, putting away the car. If I rushed, maybe I could be safely in a hot bath before he came in. I didn't want him to hassle me about ballet tonight. I pushed my doorkey into the cold lock.

In the front hall only Mama welcomed me. Thank heavens. My father had let her off at the kitchen door before he put away the car. In her arms I smelled the faint lilac scent that always seemed to seep from her pores. The amber hall light shone on her hair, making soft highlights in it the color of the copper vase by the fireplace. I wished my hair was like hers, instead of carrot-red like my father's.

"Here you are," she said, her voice careful and

gentle. "I saw your friend Doug for a minute in the foyer. He said he would find you and bring you home. I knew he would."

She smoothed at my hair that the wind had frizzed into tangled lamb's wool. I pulled off my scarf.

"Don't worry about my hair, Mama. I'll wash it or something tomorrow. Now I just want a hot bath."

Mama nodded and gave me her faint, tired, understanding smile.

"Of course, Maggie."

I dragged my ballet bag down the hall. Mama followed.

"I saw Joyce backstage," she said. "She told me a little about tonight. How disappointing for you, honey! And that Bellermont girl was awful in your part."

"I don't want to talk about it now, Mama. I just want a bath."

"Well, Maggie, your father wants to talk to you."

"Not tonight. I'm too tired to be hassled tonight."

"Well, you know how he feels about ballet. And it does put unnatural stresses on your body, which worries him. It also bothers him that it keeps you from having a normal life of family, friends, and school."

I kicked my ballet bag ahead of me.

"What's normal?" I cried. "So ballet takes a lot of time. What's time? Ballet's the most important thing in the world to me. If he stopped me from dancing, I'd die. I'd run away. I don't know what I'd do."

Mama picked up my ballet bag.

"I know," she said, sighing. "I'll put your practice clothes in the washer-dryer so they'll be ready for class in the morning."

I sighed, too. And I didn't want to think about class

34

tomorrow. Or the weekend *Nutcracker* performances. But I had to.

"And would you take care of my toe shoes too, please, Mama? They're all smelly and damp, and the ribbons need sewing."

Mama nodded.

"Did your blister bother you much?"

"No, not really. I only danced in the first act."

My blister stung now, though. And if I stood here talking to Mama much longer, my father would arrive. I hurried down the hall.

Halfway to my bedroom, I heard the kitchen door slam. My father's voice boomed.

"Has she come in yet?"

I ran the rest of the way to my room, where I tore off my clothes. I dropped them in a pile at my feet.

In the kitchen Mama murmured something, but I couldn't make out what she said. I had no trouble, however, understanding my father when he boomed again.

"I don't care if she is tired. Or disappointed. Or whatever you say she is. I want to talk to her."

I grabbed my white bathrobe off the floor and put it on. If only I could make it to the bathroom without meeting my father.

But he was coming down the hall right now. I felt rather than heard him. The carpet swallowed the sound of his footsteps, but their tramp shook the floorboards underneath. He pounded on my door.

"Maggie, I want to talk to you."

I stood in my white bathrobe waiting. I folded my arms across my chest.

"Maggie!" he shouted again.

My mother murmured out in the hall. "Why don't you talk to her in the morning? When she's rested?"

35

"Because I have to be at the hospital before she's up. Then I have a tennis match. Besides, I want to talk to her now."

The door rattled again.

"Maggie, open the door."

I shook back my hair and squeezed my arms tighter across my chest.

"Well, the door's not locked!" I said.

It flew open and the doorway filled with my father's square frame. Which, fortunately, I didn't inherit, or I could never have been a dancer. I saw his quick green eyes, yellow-splotched like mine, glare at the mess in my room. His face reddened. His pale orange eyebrows met in a frown.

"Just look at this place!" he said. "I suppose it's a pigpen because you don't have the energy to clean it, after dancing yourself to exhaustion."

Behind my father's back, Mama placed a finger on her lips. She needn't have bothered. After living with my father for fourteen years, I knew enough to keep quiet. Most of the time, that is.

He strode into my room kicking a path through my clothes and books and records. I held myself with my arms, watching his shiny, square shoes wade across my floor.

"This place is a disgrace," he said. "I want your bed made and your clothes picked up. All of them. Before you go to bed. Do I make myself clear?"

I shook back my hair and watched his foot push aside my things. I bit my lips.

"Answer me," he said.

With as little motion as possible, I nodded my head. He turned to Mama.

"And I don't want you doing it for her. It's too bad if she's worn out from ballet. She needs to grow up

36

and become responsible. You spoil her, wait on her hand and foot. She's to do it herself, Elizabeth. Do I make myself clear?"

My mother's face paled, which it does when she's angry instead of burning red as mine and my father's do. She barely moved her lips.

"Perfectly clear," she said.

"And she's not to leave this house in the morning until this room is clean," he went on.

Mama interrupted. "But she has a class."

"That's what I want to talk about, all those damned ballet classes and rehearsals and hours of torturing her tendons and ligaments. She's putting incredible strains on her body. Not to mention on our family. We never see her. That's why I insist that we have dinner together, the three of us, no matter how long we have to wait for Maggie."

I squeezed my chest to keep from answering back. As if he never got home late from the hospital!

"Then, tonight," my father continued, "she didn't even come out to join us after the ballet. I'd like an explanation about that, Maggie."

I squeezed my arms tighter across my chest and stared at the carpet. I could feel the force of his rigid square body.

"Answer me!" he said. "Couldn't you have gone out with us for dessert and spent half an hour with your family? Instead of running off with some boy?"

I broke. I flung my arms wide and shouted as loud as he had shouted.

"Yes. That's right. I did let Doug drive me home. And do you want to know why? So I wouldn't be around for you to hassle me about ballet."

I dodged past him and Mama and rushed down the hall to the bathroom. I slammed and locked the door.

Out in the hall Mama murmured, "Let her alone now, Will. She's worn out."

"It's all this damned dancing," my father said. "Exercise in moderation is one thing. After all, I play a fair amount of tennis. But this ballet thing is ridiculous and getting worse!"

Flinging off my bathrobe, I slid into the tub. I twisted open the faucet until the rush of water shut out his shouting.

Chapter Six

That weekend, Mrs. Bellermont did try to persuade McMichael to let Cynthia dance my role. But he kept his promise to me. I danced Rose in all the weekend performances of the *Nutcracker*.

I even received a line of praise in the local paper.

"Promising young local dancer Maggie Adams won well-deserved applause for her soaring jumps and graceful technique."

Mama underlined the paragraph and left the clipping on the kitchen table for my father.

"So what does that reviewer know?" I heard my father ask. "He's hardly the critic for the *New York Times*."

But the notice excited Lupe. She pinned it to the ballet school's bulletin board. From which it promptly disappeared.

"And I know who took it!" Lupe declared, one Saturday soon after New Year's.

Lupe, Joyce, and I relaxed at a little round table in the doughnut shop across the street from the ballet school. We felt tired but purified after sweating through two good hard classes.

"*Por dios*," Lupe continued. "That Mrs. Bellermont took the newspaper clipping. She can't stand anyone but her daughter to get praise. That woman's a devil!"

Joyce laughed.

"Speaking of the devil, he must have put this doughnut shop here to tempt us. Lupe's the only one who resists."

Joyce bit into her lemon-filled doughnut and I stared guiltily at mine. As usual, Lupe had nothing but a glass of water.

I sighed.

"And she's the only one thin enough to eat doughnuts."

Across the table from me she slowly sipped her water. Actually, she was too thin. And getting thinner. In practice clothes her chest and back showed the shape of each rib.

"Lupe," I said, "you're too skinny."

She glared at me and grasped her St. Christopher medal.

"*Madre mîa*, do you want me to get fat like my mother and sisters and aunts? I want to be a dancer and dancers have to be thin or the lines of their dancing don't look clean. And their partners can't lift them."

"But you're overdoing it," I said.

Joyce nodded.

"Mag's right. If you don't eat properly, you won't have the energy to dance. I noticed that you left class before toe work this afternoon."

To my surprise, tears glistened in Lupe's eyes.

"I didn't leave because I was tired!" Lupe said hotly. "I hurt my ankle. In that last combination, you had to change directions too fast. I got off-balance. Didn't you think it was hard?"

Joyce shrugged and bit into her doughnut.

Well, maybe Joyce was willing to let Lupe change the subject, but I wasn't.

"I'll bet you didn't have anything to eat today," I said. "No breakfast. No nothing."

Lupe's dark eyes glittered. She flung back her long thick hair.

"You sound like my mother. What she expects me to eat are chili and beans. All the time. Mountains of them. And turn into a mountain like Tia Guadalupe, down in Mexico. Mama's favorite sister, who I'm named after. No, thank you!"

She took a quick sip of water and choked. Joyce patted her on the back.

"Take it easy, Lupe. It's just that we're worried about you. Thirteen is awfully young to diet as much as you do."

Lupe frowned at Joyce.

"Then you want me to get fat, too. Fat like Tia! Eat all those beans and tortillas. My family can't afford salads and steak like yours can, you know."

Joyce and I stared at the table. Lupe was telling us that she was poor and this idea made us uncomfortable. I knew that McMichael spotted Lupe a few years ago in a playground dance class at the civic center. He began giving her free lessons. Now her classes were paid for by a scholarship from New York. But so were mine. I hadn't known she was poor. Until now I never even thought about whether she was rich or poor. She was just Lupe.

Finally Joyce touched Lupe's tiny waist.

"I'm sorry we've upset you, Lupe. Chili and beans are good food. They have lots of vitamins. Just eat small amounts and you'll be okay. At your age you have to eat right because you're just starting to develop."

Lupe glanced quickly down at her chest which was even flatter than mine.

"Not me," she said. "I'm still as flat as my sister Juana, who's only six."

"You'll fill out," Joyce said.

Lupe shook her head.

"And I haven't had a period for months and months."

Joyce leaned toward her.

"Don't worry. When you first start, lots of times your periods are irregular. But it's important to eat right."

Lupe nodded but still grasped her St. Christopher.

"All the same, I won't get like Tía Guadalupe. Or," she said, glancing toward the doughnut counter, "like Cynthia."

I looked up to see Cynthia Bellermont coming toward our table. On a plate, like jewels on a cushion, she carried three jelly-filled doughnuts.

Joyce moved her chair closer to Lupe's to make room for Cynthia.

"Sit down," Joyce said. "And have a doughnut. Or two. Or three."

Cynthia tilted her turned-up nose even higher.

"Well, Mommy only let me have half a grapefruit this morning so I'm starving."

Joyce laughed. "We've just been talking about diets. So your mother put you on one, did she?"

Cynthia could only nod because her mouth was

full. Raspberry filling oozed down her chin. Lupe looked away and I wondered if she were hungry or disgusted.

Joyce clicked her tongue. "If you're supposed to be on a diet, Cyn, I sure hope your mother doesn't find you here."

Cynthia glanced hastily across the busy downtown street to the ballet school, whose broad front windows gleamed in the afternoon sunlight.

"She's at a meeting over there with the Auxiliary and McMichael. So she won't find out I'm here. Unless you tell."

We shook our heads.

"Don't worry," I said. "If you want to stuff yourself, be our guest."

Staring at the flat-roofed ballet school, I wondered what McMichael and the Auxiliary were discussing over there. Or rather, what McMichael was discussing with Mrs. Bellermont because she, after all, was the Auxiliary. I asked Cynthia.

Instead of answering, she tilted her nose and swung her river of blond hair.

"It's private. Wouldn't you like to know!"

I snorted. I mean, how do you talk to a person like Cynthia? She's my age, but acts about ten.

Joyce knew how to handle Cynthia though.

"It's that important, huh, Cyn?"

Cynthia nodded, swinging her hair.

"Uh, huh."

"Then I'll bet your mother didn't tell even you what they're talking about."

"She did so! It's about the Regional Festival next June. They're deciding if the ballet we do for the Adjudicator should be choreographed by a student. Like Mommy wants."

43

Cynthia clapped her hand over her mouth.

"You tricked me!"

Joyce laughed.

"Don't worry about it, Cyn, we'll never breathe a word."

Suddenly Joyce frowned.

"But it is surprisingly generous of your mom."

I thought so, too. To let a student choreograph our entry for the festival was completely out of character for Mrs. B.

Joyce finished her doughnut.

"I wonder how McMichael feels about this," she said. "He's used to grinding out a new ballet every year for the Festival. But maybe he believes, as I do, that regional companies need to develop choreographers. Not just dancers."

She smiled.

"And I just happen to have a great idea for a ballet."

I leaned toward her. Joyce had choreographed some really neat little dances for our school demonstrations.

Cynthia's eyes widened. They glittered like blue glass.

"I really think Mommy has decided on the ballet already," she said, pursing her mouth into a little red heart.

We started to question her but stopped at the sound of a bellow from the shop's entrance.

"Cynthia Anne! You were told to wait in the Lincoln."

Mrs. Bellermont barged toward us.

Unlike my mother, this woman looked her age and older. Her breasts and belly met where her waistline should have been. And wrapped around her body, like thread around a bobbin, her polyester dress bloomed with iridescent flowers.

"You know you're forbidden in this place, Cynthia!"

Mrs. Bellermont glared at Joyce, Lupe, and me.

"But judging by all the other empty plates, I guess you're not entirely to blame. I'll thank you girls not to tempt my daughter. Now, honey, let's go. I have good news for you!"

Mrs. Bellermont dragged Cynthia to the door. I stared after them. Too much back-combing had turned Mrs. B's hairdo into a cloud of ginger-colored cotton candy. And Cynthia's blond waterfall reached nearly to her knees.

Joyce sighed.

"Poor old Cyn. I'm glad she finished her doughnuts before Mommy arrived. All three of them."

Chapter Seven

We didn't learn Mrs. Bellermont's good news until
Monday. And, as we should have known, it turned
out to be good news only for Cynthia. For Joyce,
Lupe, and me, it was bad.

On Monday when I arrived at the ballet school for
class, I saw posted on the bulletin board in the foyer
the bad news. Felt-penned in colors that matched
Mrs. Bellermont's print dresses, a notice announced:

Tryouts
Next Saturday
for
SNOW PRINCESS
Choreographed by
Cynthia Anne Bellermont

"I don't believe it!" I exclaimed, just as McMichael,
mopping sweat from his neck, walked out of class.

In the foyer, which also served as waiting room and office, a half-dozen mothers sat along two battered sofas. One woman darned a pair of tights for her daughter. Another sewed ribbons on toe shoes. Warming up for the next class, a dozen students in pink tights and black leotards clutched door frames, the desk, a chair back, and the post of a brass floor lamp. One even clung to the wooden brace that supported a tall, straggly rubber plant.

At my exclamation, the students swarmed around McMichael.

"What don't you believe, my dear?" he asked.

"This!" I jabbed a finger at the notice.

"Cynthia has a hard enough time even remembering the combinations you give in class," I continued. "How could she put together an entire ballet?"

With his towel McMichael mopped sweat from his balding head. He had just finished teaching an intermediate class.

"Be a little tolerant, Maggie. You haven't seen it. It's really not so bad."

I glared. "Have you seen it?"

He nodded. "The main parts. For a fourteen-year-old, it's not bad. It's sort of a cross between City Ballet's *Snow Maiden* and a traditional second act of *Swan Lake.* But with a little strengthening and rearranging..."

I stamped my foot.

"You mean, you'll redo it for her."

He rubbed his head with his towel. He looked tired and had two more classes to teach that night. But I kept at him.

"Just because her mother's Auxiliary President—"

"Mrs. Bellermont has a valid argument, Maggie,"

McMichael said. "Regional companies should develop young choreographers."

I nodded. "I agree. So does Joyce. And she has a great ballet. But you didn't give her a chance."

Raising his scraggly eyebrows, he looked interested.

"I didn't know she had one. Is it good?"

I had to admit that I hadn't seen it.

"But you know the variations she does for the demonstrations."

He nodded. "Excellent. Some are highly innovative."

"So how come you told Mrs. Bellermont yes, you'd put on her daughter's ballet—which has got to be mainly Mrs. B's?"

McMichael scrubbed at his head.

"Maybe. Maybe not. Maybe she made a suggestion here or there. But, after all, she knows ballet. She wanted to be a dancer herself. She even studied with Nijinska."

"Well," I said doubtfully. "If the ballet is hers, she should say so. And not claim that Cynthia did it. And if you're in favor of developing young choreographers, how about developing Joyce?"

McMichael sighed. "I wish I had known. Now it's all been decided."

"Decided by Mrs. Bellermont—that's who decided it," I cried. "It's not fair. Joyce didn't get a chance. We should have had a choreography contest!"

I rushed out of the foyer and into the long narrow dressing room. The odor of cologne and sweat hung in here like the trails of ground fog that on some mornings drift above the few green fields as yet unsubdivided in our valley. I flung my ballet bag onto the yellow bench that ran along two walls of the dressing room. Yanking off my jeans and sweater, I jammed them onto a hook among the other clumps of street clothes above the bench. I sat down to pull on my tights.

After advanced class and partnering class that night I was too tired even to think about Cynthia's stupid ballet. But, hurrying through the foyer to meet Mama out in the car, I couldn't help glaring toward the announcement. It was gone. Vanished from the bulletin board!

I turned to McMichael for an explanation, but he, too, had vanished. He was only in the men's dressing room changing, I knew, but I couldn't wait. At home my father would be pacing a rut in our carpet, waiting for Mama and me and his dinner.

The first thing I noticed Tuesday afternoon when I burst into the foyer, was a new notice on the bulletin board. To read it, I didn't have to go any nearer than the front door. McMichael's thick black handwriting proclaimed:

Choreography Contest
Sponsored by the Santa Inez Regional Ballet
Auxiliary
for
New Ballets
by
Student Choreographers
Next Saturday at 3:00 P.M.
First Prize: Presentation before the Regional
    Ballet Adjudicator
Second Prize: A pair of toe shoes (new)
Third Prize: One jelly-filled doughnut

Directions for the presentation of the new ballets:

1. State name of ballet, music, and composer
2. Present plot outline
3. List and describe roles
4. Diagram major groupings
5. Play tape of selected music
6. Demonstrate main variations

I was so excited I could hardly breathe. Coming into the foyer behind me, Joyce stood in the doorway, laughing.

"Good old McMichael!"

I shook my head in disbelief.

"How do you suppose he managed?"

Joyce clapped an arm around my shoulders.

"Over Mrs. B's dead body! Just remember, Mag, McMichael's artistic director. If he really wants something, he gets it. If he didn't, Mommy would have Cynthia dancing all your lovely solos. And wouldn't that be a catastrophe!"

I raised my eyebrows. I hadn't thought of that.

"I guess he really wanted your ballet to have a chance. I hope it's good."

She laughed. "Of course, it's good. It's called *Golden Shoes*."

I clapped my hands together.

"Sounds great! Do I get a part?"

Joyce giggled and, with her arm still around me, dragged me to the dressing room door.

"Only the Sugarplum Fairy," she said. "Just old Sugarplum."

I stopped. I squealed.

"You're kidding. You've got Sugarplum in your ballet?"

She nodded. "Just for you."

Suddenly, I bit my lip.

"I just had an awful thought, Joyce. Who's going to judge the contest?"

She stopped with one hand on the door knob.

"I don't know," she said, suddenly quiet. "It'll make a difference, won't it?"

I nodded and crossed my fingers.

Chapter Eight

It turned out that we needn't have worried about the judges. But we didn't know that at 3:00 P.M., Saturday, the time announced for the choreography contest, when Joyce, Lupe, and I sat on the smoothly planed floor of the classroom, stretching our turnouts.

Our legs angled out. The soles of our feet touched. Swathed in thick woolen tights, legwarmers, our legs beat up and down like heavy triangular wings.

"I might as well face it," Joyce said. "I'll never have a decent turnout like you two. And without a good turnout, I'll never have good lines. Look at this."

With her hands, she pushed down hard on her knees but they remained at least six inches from the floor.

Two members of the Auxiliary, without Mrs. Bellermont, clattered on high heels into the classroom. They creaked onto folding chairs—the only furniture in the room, unless you counted the old upright piano, the tape recorder, the two big mirrors shining at the front of the room, and the wooden ballet barre.

McMichael strode into the classroom and immediately opened the double doors that let onto the school's unpaved parking lot. We had finished class only fifteen minutes before, so the odor of cologne and sweat still hung in the close, humid air.

"Needs a little airing out, doesn't it?" he said. "That should help. And now I have an announcement: There will be no contest after all. I've received only one entry, Joyce Mallory's *Golden Shoes*, which, fortunately, the Auxiliary and I like very much."

Everyone gasped except the Auxiliary members on their creaking chairs at the front of the classroom. Lupe and I hugged Joyce. But she was frowning.

"What happened to Cynthia's ballet?" she asked.

McMichael scrubbed his hand through his hair.

"The Bellermont ballet has been withdrawn," he said.

Joyce jumped up.

"Why? And where are they—Mrs. B. and Cynthia? Cyn didn't show up for class this morning either."

McMichael cleared his throat.

"They're out of town."

Lupe and I looked at each other. Joyce continued to frown.

"What's going on?" she asked.

McMichael shook his head.

"It's not important. Let's get on with your ballet. Tell us about it."

Still frowning, Joyce walked to the front of the room.

"Well," she began slowly, "my ballet's based on a really old theme. In fact, the Greeks used it three or four thousand years ago."

I leaned forward. Once Joyce told me she was really into Greek myths and plays. She wished she knew classical Greek so that she could read the dramas in the original language.

Gradually Joyce's frown smoothed away.

"The gimmick in both the myth and in my ballet is a contest," she said. "In the Greek story there's a beauty contest between three goddesses. The prize is a golden apple."

I nodded. I knew the story. In fact, a ballet called *Helen of Troy* used the plot. Was Joyce's ballet another *Helen of Troy?*

Joyce paced up and down. I watched her reflection in the mirrors and couldn't help thinking what a shame that her stocky build is out of favor these days with ballet companies, who like long, supple bodies like mine.

"In my ballet," Joyce said, "three contestants dance for a pair of golden shoes."

I gasped. Now I understood where the Sugarplum Fairy came in. Joyce smiled.

"You're way ahead of me, Mag. As you've already guessed, the three contestants are Sleeping Beauty, the Swan Queen, and Mag's dream role—the Sugarplum Fairy. And guess who wins the Golden Shoes?"

I waved my hand as if I were in school.

"Sugarplum," I cried. "Of course, Sugarplum."

Joyce shook her head.

"Unfortunately, things are a little underhanded in

my ballet just as they were in the Greek myth. There, the winner bribed the judge by promising him Helen, the most beautiful woman in the world."

Joyce paused and looked at us all. Now she seemed to be enjoying herself.

"In my ballet, after awarding the Golden Shoes, the judge takes off his beard and turns out to be Prince Charming. The winner, of course, is Sleeping Beauty."

We all clapped.

"But it's unfair," I cried. "We didn't have a chance, the Swan Queen and I."

Joyce shrugged.

"That's how contests are. Right, Mr. McMichael?"

McMichael rubbed his head.

"There was no contest, my dear. Your ballet was uncontested. And before we see some of your variations, I'd like to remind you that as artistic director of the company, I retain the right to choose the cast."

By the way he scrubbed at his forehead, I knew he was pretty nervous. Joyce shrugged.

"That's okay. I've only promised one role and I know you won't object—Mag as Sugarplum."

What followed I couldn't believe. McMichael shook his head.

"I'm sorry, but that role's promised to someone else."

Joyce stared at him.

"To whom?"

He coughed.

"I'd rather not say right now."

Joyce planted her hands on her hips.

"Cynthia Bellermont, I bet. Her mother's wanted her in that role for years."

I sat quietly, staring at the dark smooth floor. It looked like I'd never get to dance Sugarplum. Lupe put her arms around me. Joyce folded hers across her chest.

"Now I understand," she said. "You got Mrs. Bellermont to withdraw Cynthia's ballet in exchange for the Sugarplum role."

McMichael sighed.

"That's about it, I'm afraid. The Adjudicator would never put the Bellermont ballet in the Regional Festival. It's too trite, too amateurish. And if yours is staged and danced well, it has a good chance not only of making the Festival, but of being chosen for the Gala."

Joyce jutted her chin.

"Mag does Sugarplum or we don't do my ballet. Period."

McMichael cleared his throat.

"Maggie can have her pick of the other roles, but this is the arrangement I made with Mrs. Bellermont."

Joyce glared.

"I won't compromise at Mag's expense."

I sat very still. Sugarplum was my dream role, but Joyce's ballet would go to the festival and allow us all to perform there. Besides, Joyce's Sugarplum wasn't the real Sugarplum.

I stood up.

"I'd really like to do Sugarplum, Joyce, but I'd almost as soon dance the Swan Queen."

Joyce eyed me.

"Are you sure, Mag?"

I shrugged.

"After all, they're both good roles," I said.

McMichael sighed.

"Thank heavens, that's settled. And for Sleeping Beauty, if you agree, Joyce, I suggest Lupe. The role of the judge goes to Chris, of course."

McMichael's "of course" meant that, except for an occasional visiting professional, Chris was the only male student in the advanced class. In fact, unless you counted two ten-year-old beginners who took ballet because their sisters did, Chris was the only male student in the school.

McMichael laid an arm around Joyce's shoulders.

"I'm so happy that everything's settled," he said. "Now let's see your variations, Joyce."

Chapter Nine

McMichael might consider Joyce's ballet all settled, but Lupe and I, and the choreographer herself, felt unsettled about a number of details.

"I sure will have to simplify that Sugarplum variation!" Joyce said later that afternoon in the doughnut shop. She and I each ordered our favorites while Lupe asked for her usual glass of water.

"Cynthia can't even do decent double *pirouettes,* let alone those triples and quadruples I put in for Mag."

At a table near the window I bit into my raspberry-filled doughnut.

"You certainly did give Sugarplum a lot of turns and big jumps," I said.

"Of course. I designed the role for you. Your turns and leaps are light and sure. I never dreamed we'd end up with poor old Cynthia in the role."

I licked drips of raspberry jelly from my fingers

and wondered how to tell Joyce, tactfully of course, that I found the Swan Queen variation a trifle dull.

"I suppose you'll give the Swan Queen a few *pirouettes* and *grands jetés*, now that I'm dancing the role," I said.

Joyce shook her head.

"No way, Mag. They wouldn't be in keeping with the character. She's elegant and icy cold. A snow queen really. That's why I have all those slow *développés* and *arabesques*. Things that'll show off your long body and gorgeous feet."

I shrugged. I hoped she knew what she was doing. Lupe sipped her water.

"What about my variation?" she asked. "Do you think I can do all those quick little beats you gave Sleeping Beauty?"

"Of course, Lupe. My Sleeping Beauty is very young and small and quick. Like you. She runs and plays in a sunny garden. Does lots of *glissades* and neat little beats. Which you do beautifully."

Lupe fingered her St. Christopher.

"Which I used to do. Now I get so tired."

Joyce frowned.

"You don't eat enough, Lupe. You'll get sick."

"*Por dios*! I'm not going to listen to all that again. Anyway, I have to catch my bus."

Flinging back her chair, she hurried to the door. Her long dark hair looked too heavy for her thin little body. Joyce shook her head.

"I'm worried about Lupe. She's so afraid of getting fat. Fat? She must weigh all of ninety pounds!"

Joyce and I left soon afterwards. Joyce's bus came first and, as she climbed on, who should amble off, but Doug.

Since the night I almost danced Sugarplum, I had

only seen him occasionally passing between classes at school. And when I did spot him in a hallway, he usually walked beside a tall pretty girl who constantly flattered him with a lovely braces-free smile.

Now he alighted from the bus and I smiled at him, careful to keep my lips closed over my braces. He grinned. His Adam's apple bounced up and down his throat.

"Gosh, Mag, it's good to see you. How have you been?"

"Fine, Doug."

He glanced at my ballet bag.

"Still doing the ballet bit, I see."

I nodded.

"And you're still into basketball, I suppose."

"Oh, sure. Most afternoons. Say, how come I never see you around school?"

My face grew hot. Did he know I avoided him when I saw him with that girl? No, he seemed honestly to want to know why he hadn't seen me.

"Well, I'm only at school in the mornings," I said. "I have four solids from 8:00 A.M. until noon. And I'm excused from PE. So my afternoons are free."

"Good deal!" he said. "But why no PE? I mean, you're perfectly healthy, aren't you?"

I nodded.

"Oh, I'm healthy enough. And my ballet teacher wants me to stay that way. And uninjured. He thinks regular PE can harm a dancer's body. At school, you usually don't warm up your muscles well enough before you start something strenuous."

Doug raised an eyebrow.

"He may have a point, but in basketball we do a good warmup before a game or practice."

I shrugged. "Well, anyway, that's what McMi-

61

chael thinks. He also says that dancers shouldn't do certain exercises or sports because they develop muscles that interfere with ballet. Besides, who needs PE? My daily ballet classes give me plenty of exercise."

He nodded. "I can imagine! So what do you do afternoons?"

I smiled. "What do you think?"

We wagged our heads, laughing.

"Ballet!" we chorused.

He took my hand and swung it.

"No kidding, though, Mag, we should try getting together again. We really hit it off. Maybe you have some spare time now that you've finished that Christmas ballet."

I glanced up at his long friendly face. I saw his soft, springy curls against the greenish late afternoon sky. Maybe he wasn't attached to that girl, after all. In a way, though, I was the one attached, firmly attached to ballet.

"Well, I still take a lot of lessons and things, Doug."

Past the corner where we stood, the late traffic hooted and snorted home to the suburbs. Doug leaned down so that I could hear him above the noise of the cars.

"A friend of mine's giving a party next Friday night. How about coming with me, Mag?"

I forgot about ballet and about my braces. I really smiled at him.

"Sure. I'd like that," I said. Then I remembered that McMichael had scheduled the first rehearsal of *Golden Shoes* for Friday night. If I skipped it without a good reason, I could be kicked out of the company. Besides I would hate to miss a rehearsal.

"I'd really like to go, Doug, but we're rehearsing a new ballet. I have to be there."

Doug twisted his hands behind him.

"Same old problem, huh, Mag? Well, it's been nice talking to you. See you around."

He saluted me with a quick snap of hand to forehead and sauntered into the crowd. I watched his lanky body sway away from me. My throat swelled with an awful ache. Here he was, leaving me again.

A few minutes later my bus arrived to carry me home in time for dinner at six, which my father considered the reasonable hour to dine. As if his crazy schedule never caused our late meals!

Chapter Ten

We didn't have dinner that night at six because my father came home from a tennis match at 6:30. By the time he showered, it was seven. And by that time the baked chicken breasts were dried out.

My father laid down his fork.

"The chicken's overdone," he said.

Mama went on eating.

"Yes. And dinner's an hour late."

I expected him to explode, but he must have won the tennis match and been feeling good, because he only arched his orange eyebrows and nodded.

"I'm sorry I'm late. But it's not often, not every night. And I do think it's important for us to have dinner together. As a family."

After rehearsals began for *Golden Shoes*, I almost never got home for dinner with my family. At six or at any other time. By serving his favorite meals with wine and lighted candles, though, Mama convinced my father most nights that they could dine without me. He also calmed down about the amount of time I spent on ballet. Maybe he had decided he couldn't do anything about it. Or maybe he was just awfully busy at the hospital and at his office, and didn't notice how much I was dancing. Anyway, things seemed smoother at home.

Not at rehearsals, though. Before we had even started one of the first ones, Mrs. Bellermont pranced into the classroom on platform shoes. It was nearly nine o'clock and dark outside, and the studio's fluorescent lamps reflected from the transoms that let in light and air along the top of two of the walls.

Exhausted from class, dancers draped themselves, limp as their damp towels, against the *barre*. Chris and the two boys he had recruited from a nearby college mopped sweat from their necks and shoulders. Sitting on the floor in leg warmers, Lupe and I stretched our turnouts. I could hear Joyce and McMichael talking in the foyer.

Mrs. Bellermont smoothed her bright skirts and settled herself on a folding chair between the mirrors.

"What's holding things up?" she asked. "I thought rehearsals began at 8:30 sharp."

Nobody answered. I stretched until my face rested against one shin. Good Lord, was she going to watch the entire rehearsal?

She crossed one fat leg over the other.

"And where's Cynthia?" she asked.

Lupe and I exchanged glances. We knew exactly where Cynthia was. She had put a coat over her practice clothes and crossed the street to the doughnut shop.

Mrs. Bellermont tapped the toe of one shoe on the floor.

"Well, has the cat got everybody's tongue? Maggie, where's Cynthia?"

Now, I'm no friend of Cynthia's, but I feel a little sorry for her. With a mother like that.

"I don't know, Mrs. Bellermont."

At that moment Cynthia herself stomped in, stuffing in the last bite of doughnut. Mrs. Bellermont sprang up and teetered toward her.

"Cynthia Anne Bellermont!"

Cynthia's eyes widened with alarm. Wiping her sugary fingers down the sides of her tights, she edged toward the *barre*.

Mrs. Bellermont clattered after her.

"Where's your will power, Cynthia Anne?" she asked. "And where's Ian McMichael?"

McMichael strolled in with Joyce. Mrs. Bellermont rushed to him.

"Ian, I think the company should forbid members to go to the doughnut shop. Then Cynthia wouldn't be tempted."

McMichael shrugged. Joyce smirked.

"Let's ask the city to change the zoning regulations," she said. "Forbid any doughnut, ice cream, or candy shop within two blocks of a ballet school."

Mrs. Bellermont glanced at her.

"Do you think they would?" she asked uncertainly.

Joyce didn't answer, but Lupe and I sputtered, trying to keep from laughing.

Catching on, Mrs. Bellermont stamped one of her platforms.

"Very funny! Don't give yourself airs, Joyce Mallory, just because you think you're a big-time choreographer."

Ignoring her, Joyce snapped a cassette into the tape recorder. She motioned us to gather around.

67

"We'll learn the Swan Queen's entrance tonight," she said. "Ready, Mag?"

I think Joyce decided to work on my role just to spite Mrs. Bellermont.

Sure enough, Mrs. Bellermont glared at me.

"Well, if you're working with Maggie tonight, I might as well take Cynthia home."

Joyce eyed the woman. Boy, did I wish I had Joyce's courage!

"I need Cynthia here," Joyce said. "At this point in the ballet she's on stage reacting to the Swan Queen's entrance."

Mrs. Bellermont crossed her arms.

"She can pick that up later," she said. "Why should she wait around now for a little pantomime?"

"It's more than pantomime. She dances with the corps."

Mrs. Bellermont's eyes shot open.

"The corps? But Cynthia's a principal."

"Not in this scene," Joyce said.

She seemed less interested in Mrs. Bellermont, though, than in getting on with the rehearsal. She chalked an x on the floor.

"This is where the Swan Queen stops, Mag. Okay?"

But Mrs. Bellermont refused to be put off. She appealed to McMichael.

"Ian, I'm taking Cynthia home. She's not needed here tonight."

McMichael rubbed his head.

"What about it, Joyce?" he asked. "Is Cynthia really necessary tonight?"

Joyce nodded firmly.

"Yes. I've already explained why."

McMichael shrugged.

"Then Cynthia stays. But you can go, Jean," he told Mrs. Bellermont. "I'll see that Cynthia gets home safely."

Mrs. Bellermont glared.

"If Cynthia stays, I stay."

She flounced back to her chair. I wanted to cheer. Joyce turned to me.

"Watch," she said, posing. "I want your head and back and neck lifted, lifted. Like this. My Swan Queen is haughty, haughty and cold."

I imitated Joyce.

"Good!" she said. "Head a little higher."

In the doorway McMichael nodded.

"Pretend someone's lifting you up from behind the ears."

I stretched higher.

"Exactly!" Joyce said. "That's it. Now the entrance. Line up by the door. Everyone except Chris and Cynthia, who are front left. And Lupe hasn't entered yet."

We gathered where Joyce pointed.

"Okay, Mag, in front, between Gus and John. This time they're your escorts. Imagine they've put white swan feathers in their caps. Lightly rest your fingertips on their wrists. Lightly. Lightly."

Mrs. Bellermont interrupted.

"Why does Maggie have two partners?" she asked, pointing to Gus and John, the college boys Chris found for the ballet.

"They escort all three contestants," Joyce said.

Mrs. Bellermont frowned.

"Won't that look funny, having the same two boys escort all three dancers?"

Joyce nodded.

"Could be. But Chris is the judge, and, as usual,

there are not enough boys to go around. And," she added, smiling at John and Gus, "we're very glad to find some men with dance training."

"I understood they were modern dancers, not ballet dancers," Mrs. Bellermont said.

Joyce shrugged.

"So? They've had training. That's the important thing. Now let's get on with it."

Mrs. Bellermont grunted but stopped talking.

Joyce beckoned to the corps girls.

"Now you six—line up by threes. You'll have changed from the lollypop hats you wore to enter with Sugarplum, into white winged swan caps. Line up directly behind Mag and the boys. That's right."

Joyce smiled her approval.

"Okay, now this is the Swan Queen's promenade. Remember, Mag, keep the haughty posture I showed you. The rest of you ham it up, exaggerate it. Like this. It's all the promenades in all the court scenes in all the classic ballets."

Joyce demonstrated the promenade, smiling, dipping, bending. She was really funny. Everyone in the room laughed except Mrs. Bellermont.

"And what's Cynthia supposed to be doing way over on the other side of the stage?" she asked. "Twiddling her thumbs?"

Joyce turned her back on Mrs. Bellermont, but went over to Cynthia.

"Cyn, while the Swan Queen's entering, you waltz half time to the music, circling with Chris. And flirt with him. Flirt like mad. He's the Judge, after all, and you want to win."

Joyce turned on the tape recorder.

"Okay, Swan Queen, cold and haughty."

Lifting my head high, I led the group to the center

70

of the classroom. In the mirror I saw my reflection. Slim, straight—I was a queen, despite my stretched and faded leg warmers and my red hair burning under the fluorescent lamps.

I glanced at Joyce. She nodded.

"Great, Mag! That's it!"

A chair creaked at the front of the room. McMichael sat down beside Mrs. Bellermont. Leaning toward him, she shrieked with high false laughter. She made sure I could hear what she whispered.

"Ridiculous, isn't it, Ian. A Swan Queen with braces on her teeth."

Chapter Eleven

The next morning Mama called my orthodontist. When he saw me he made his usual corny jokes.

"With rings on her fingers and braces on her teeth, Maggie shall dance wherever she goes."

"I'm serious," I told him. "When do I get them off?"

"I'm serious too," he said. "We'll remove them when I think a retainer is sufficient to hold the placement."

Which meant I would have to dance Swan Queen for the Adjudicator with my braces glittering.

At rehearsal that night I complained to Joyce.

"Well, keep your mouth shut," she said, sorting through her collection of cassettes. "This Swan Queen doesn't smile anyway. She's cold as ice. Now I want Sleeping Beauty's variation. Center stage, Lupe," Joyce called.

Snapping a cassette into the tape recorder, she faced us.

"Chris, John, Gus, front left. You six corps girls line up rear left on the diagonal I chalked. Swan Queen and Sugarplum, in front of them. That's right. Now, where's Lupe?"

She looked around and then went on with her instructions.

"I want exaggerated admiration from the corps girls. Ohs and ahs in mime. Ham it up. But Mag, you and Sugarplum think Sleeping Beauty stinks, right? Stay in character, though. Cyn, remember Sugarplum is simpering and sticky sweet. Where the heck did Lupe go?"

Cynthia took a sloppy fourth position beside me.

"I couldn't care less where Lupe is," she said. "And I think we should just forget this whole ballet. It's dumb, dumb, dumb! The Sugarplum Fairy should be pretty and elegant, not silly. Mommy thought that's how she would be. How could Joyce dare to change things?"

From my Swan Queen pose, I eyed Cynthia.

"It's called originality," I said.

Cynthia sniffed.

"Well, my ballet wasn't dumb like this one. Mine would have made it to the Festival for sure, probably to the Gala performance."

Joyce interrupted us.

"Have you two seen Lupe?"

We shook our heads.

"Not since she came back from getting the hamburger with us," I said.

"Well, she's vanished," Joyce said.

She peered around the room again as if she thought Lupe might be hiding behind the upright piano or under Mrs. Bellermont's flowered skirts.

74

From her creaking chair beside McMichael, Mrs. Bellermont gestured toward the door.

"I noticed her sneak out a little while ago," she said.

McMichael looked in the foyer, but shook his head.

"Mag, see if she's in the dressing room," Joyce said.

Lupe wasn't, but I heard someone in the toilet cubicle, throwing up. I hesitated.

"Lupe? Are you in there?"

No one answered, but the retching sounds continued. I tried the door. It was locked from the inside.

"Lupe? It's me, Maggie. Are you okay?"

Still no reply, but the retching stopped. I rattled the door.

"Lupe, do you need help? Shall I get Joyce or somebody?"

"No," came the faint answer.

I waited, staring at the tan door. The bottom of the door ended about a foot and a half above the floor. Should I crawl under?

When I'm sick to my stomach, I want Mama holding my head. But maybe Lupe liked being alone in there. Anyway, it made me sick to go near people vomiting. But maybe she needed help.

Fortunately, at that moment the door to the cubicle opened. Lupe crept out, holding onto the wall. Her face looked gray. Tears ran down it.

"I'm so weak," she whispered, brushing a lock of damp hair off her forehead. "It makes me sweat, being sick like that."

She felt her way along the wall and dropped onto the bench. I wet a paper towel in the basin and handed it to her. After I've been sick, I like Mama to

75

wipe my face with a damp cloth. I watched Lupe to see if she was going to throw up again.

"Do you think you've got stomach flu?" I asked, hoping I wouldn't catch it. "Has anyone else in your family had it?"

She rested her head back against the wall.

"It was that hamburger," she said faintly. "I shouldn't have eaten it."

I frowned.

"But, Lupe, you had to have something. You didn't eat all day."

She nodded.

"I didn't feel hungry today. I should have had some juice or soup instead. I keep those down okay."

"Lupe," I said, "you should see a doctor."

She leaped up. Her eyes flashed.

"Why should I see a doctor? *Por dios*, I'm not sick. I'm fine. Let's go back to the rehearsal."

Suddenly, she bent double, her head level with her knees. I rushed to her and looped my arms around her waist. I felt her hands. They were cold and damp, as if they had come from a refrigerator.

"Lupe, what's the matter? Are you going to be sick again?"

Slowly she straightened up.

"I'm just dizzy," she said with a little smile. "And—please don't say anything to Joyce or anyone. I'm fine."

I shook my head. She looked so thin, so tired.

"Are you sure? Maybe you should go home now."

She grabbed me with her cold hands.

"No, Maggie. It's nothing. Maybe I'm starting my periods again. Do you think so?"

I looked at her. Her lips were bluish-gray, as if she

had swum too long in a cold lake.

"Periods don't start like that," I said. "I think you should tell someone. Maybe I should talk to my father. He's a doctor, you know."

She grabbed me again.

"No, no, Maggie. You're my best friend. Promise you won't tell. I have to dance for the Adjudicator. Promise me."

While she begged, her great dark eyes gazed into mine. Her thin blue lips moved rapidly. Against her bony chest, she clutched her St. Christopher medal. What could I do? I promised.

Delighted, she hugged me. She kissed both my cheeks.

"*Cariña! Cariña!* Maggie! My best friend! We'll dance at the Festival together, won't we?"

I hugged her back. Who could resist her?

"Of course, Lupe."

Chapter Twelve

When I found Lupe throwing up at the ballet school, I told her we would dance at the Festival, for sure. But of course, we wouldn't know until after tonight. Tonight was Adjudication Night.

Now, in the dressing room of the rented high school auditorium, I crossed my fingers. Out front waited an invited audience which included Mama and my father. Not to mention the Adjudicator from the Regional Ballet Association. If he liked *Golden Shoes*, we would stage it at the Festival in June. If he liked it a lot, we would present it not at the Chamber Concert just for other students at the Festival, but at the Gala Concert to which the public is invited.

Joyce paced back and forth, back and forth, in the dressing room I shared with Lupe and Cynthia.

"The Adjudicator! What a title!" she said. "Why couldn't they call him the Judge? Adjudicator sounds like the Grand Inquisitor of the Middle Ages—or God!"

She stopped pacing and struck her fist against her forehead.

"I haven't time to stay here keeping up your courage. I need to check the lighting cues again. You'll all do fine. Even silly old Mag."

I started to object, but the door closed behind her.

Silly old Mag, was I? Well, tonight was practically a life-and-death matter. I had to remember a thousand things: to balance and stretch out my *penchés*, to be cold and haughty, to keep my mouth shut over my braces.

Next to me, Cynthia ladled on her eye make-up. With that much liner she'd look like an evil sorceress instead of Sugarplum.

"What are you staring at, carrot-top?" she asked, opening her eyes wide and beading on mascara.

I turned away. No need to get into a hassle with her. I had jitters enough already.

I put on my Swan Queen costume and smoothed down the crisp white tutu. The Auxiliary, under Ida's supervision, had made all new costumes for *Golden Shoes*.

Reaching back to fasten my zipper, I looked around for Lupe who usually rushed to do it for me. Not this time. She sat at the dressing table at the far end from Cynthia.

"Hey, Lupe, I need zipping," I said.

Slowly she looked at me. One hand gripped her St. Christopher.

"I can't do it, Maggie," she said.

I stared at her. I mean, zipping me up was no big deal. Why did she sound so tragic?

"That's okay, Lupe," I said. "I can zip myself."

She shook her head. Her trembling lips were as

80

blue as on the night I found her vomiting. I turned then, and really looked at her. Naked except for her pale pink tights, her little body was a delicate skeleton under a thin sheath of olive-gray skin. She had no breasts at all. The only bulges on her body were her knees, which looked a little swollen. She pushed herself up from the dressing table.

"I mean I can't do Sleeping Beauty," she said, coming to me. "Oh, Maggie, all I can remember about the steps is that they're so quick. So many little *brisés*. They make me so tired. Hold still now."

I pushed her gently away.

"It's okay, Lupe. You don't have to zip me."

But she refused to sit down.

"No, I want to. I like to. I always do it for you, Maggie. It will calm me."

She closed the zipper slowly. Half way up she stopped, then yanked the tab.

"*Por dios*, it's stuck!"

I pulled away from her.

"Are you sure?"

Taking hold of the tab, I jerked it frantically.

"Look what you've done, Lupe. You've jammed it. What'll I do now?"

At the dressing table, Cynthia turned to watch. A little smile creased her fat face.

"That's why I wait for Mommy to zip me," she said.

I glared at her.

"Nobody asked you."

I flung open the dressing room door.

"Ida," I wailed into the corridor, hoping the wardrobe mistress would hear me wherever she was. "Ida, my zipper's stuck."

In a minute Ida, plump and white-haired, scurried in, followed, unfortunately, by Mrs. Bellermont. She must have thought she was playing the old queen in *Swan Lake*. I mean, her usual flowered dress had lengthened into a floor-sweeping gown. And on top of her sprayed and back-combed hair perched a crown of green roses. I couldn't believe it!

In the center of the room, Ida looked around.

"Who's having zipper trouble?" she asked.

"Me," I said, pushing my back at her.

"So you are," she said, reaching one quick hand up under my tutu. Years ago Ida used to work as a wardrobe mistress for Ballet Theatre. She quit to get married and now volunteers with our little company.

She clicked her tongue.

"It's caught on the material. Too much seam allowance. There now, my darling, you're zipped up properly. Who else needs help?"

Cynthia bounded to her.

"Me, Ida. You can help me into my costume."

Mrs. Bellermont planted her hands on her hips.

"Why, Cynthia Anne. I'm here. You know I always dress you."

Ida laughed.

"Run along to Mommy, Cynthia, my darling. We have a little one over here who really needs my help."

I'd forgotten all about Lupe. Her head rested on the smudged top of the dressing table.

Ida touched Lupe's shoulder.

"Come, my darling, let's get you into your costume. You're our Sleeping Beauty tonight."

When Lupe raised her face, Ida clicked her tongue.

"Oh, my! You do need Ida's help!"

Staring at Lupe, I bit my lip. I must have hurt her

feelings when I scolded her for jamming my zipper. She was crying. Her face, which had been lying in a dark puddle of tears and makeup, was streaked with gray. Ida continued her comforting croon.

"Never mind, little one, Ida will fix everything. Stand up now."

Lupe stood there, drooping. I felt awful. I hadn't meant to hurt her.

Ida's quick fingers erased the gray smudges from Lupe's face and blended a delicate pink onto each cheek. She rouged Lupe's blue lips.

"Now, my darling, into your costume."

Ida slid the pale blue tutu off its hanger. Still drooping, Lupe let herself be dressed and zipped. Ida's tongue clicked again. She grasped a handful of loose material.

"Miles too big in the waist," she said. "And I fit the costume myself. You've been losing more weight, little one. Take care you don't blow away. Have you been sick?"

For an instant Lupe's glance flashed me a question. I shook my head. I hadn't told anyone about the night I found her vomiting.

Ida took needle and thread from the pincushion she wore like a bracelet on her left wrist and set to work. When she finished sewing, she patted Lupe's waist.

"There now, fits like the bark on a tree. And just in time too. There goes the bell."

After Ida left, someone rapped on the door.

"Five minutes!" Joyce called.

Cynthia swung her long hair.

"Does she think we're deaf and can't hear the bell?".

83

I glared at her.

"Joyce's just nervous," I said. "After all, it is her ballet."

Mrs. Bellermont sniffed and grabbed her daughter's arm.

"Come, Cynthia Anne. Let these girls be late if they like. But you're Sugarplum, and Sugarplum has the first entrance."

Cynthia followed her mother out the door.

Watching myself in the mirror, I did a quick circle of *bourrées en pointe*. My tutu and toe shoes fit perfectly.

"This is it," I said. "We're going to the Festival. I just know it. Maybe we'll make the Gala. Come on, Lupe."

Starting toward the door, I looked back for Lupe.

She wasn't following. She stood swaying in the middle of the room. Her fingers fluttered through the sign of the cross.

"*Madre mia*, I'm fainting," she whispered and crumpled to the floor.

Chapter Thirteen

For a second I stared at Lupe on the cold floor, wilted like a flower somebody had picked, and then dropped.

I ran to her.

"Lupe! Get up!"

I tried to lift her, but she fell back limp and heavy. Her eyes and her face, rosy with makeup, were closed.

Kneeling beside her, I yelled for help.

McMichael came first, then Joyce.

"I'll get your dad," she said. "He's out front, isn't he? In the meantime, shouldn't you cover her with something?"

McMichael grabbed my coat and Cynthia's shawl and we folded them around Lupe. To my relief, she opened her eyes. I hugged her.

"Lupe! Are you all right?"

She smiled faintly.

"Just tired," she whispered.

"Was it because of what I said?" I asked. "I was so awful about the zipper."

"It doesn't matter," she said.

Then Joyce led in my father. He stooped beside Lupe to feel her pulse. Her hand looked so small in his huge square one. She closed her eyes again. She seemed to trust him. I backed against the dressing table to be out of the way.

Right behind my father, Lupe's mother barged in. She had been in the audience, too. She tumbled to her knees, and cradled and rocked her daughter.

"Mi hija, mi poble hijita!" she wailed.

Into the doorway crowded Lupe's lean, mustached father, several sisters, two aunts, and half a dozen children. All the women were moaning and lamenting in Spanish. Joyce tried to quiet them.

"Please be quiet, so Dr. Adams can find out what's wrong."

But the family either couldn't or wouldn't understand. Finally, McMichael nudged all except the mother out into the corridor and closed the dressing room door. I heard him out there trying to explain.

Joyce turned to my father.

"Now then, Dr. Adams, what's wrong with her? Can she dance tonight?"

My father stood up, leaving Lupe to be rocked by her mother. He pulled a clean white handkerchief from his breast pocket and mopped his wide forehead.

"Looks like severe malnutrition," he said, frowning. "Probably anemia, too. The rest of the family looks well-nourished. How in the devil did she get into this condition? Just dancing couldn't have done it. She belongs in a hospital."

In spite of speaking no English, Lupe's mother seemed to recognize the word hospital.

"No hospital!" she cried, her dark eyes rolling. "No hospital!"

My father shook his head.

"I was afraid of that. A lot of the Mexicans I see don't trust doctors or hospitals."

He gestured his big hand toward the door.

"Do any of them out there speak English?" he asked. "I want to explain the seriousness of her condition."

Usually calm Joyce was pacing up and down, muttering, "What are we going to do?" so I went to the door.

I beckoned to the seventeen-year-old sister, who once in a while came to the ballet school with Lupe.

"Tonie?" I called.

The girl, who could have been Lupe's twin, only taller and plumper, darted to me. The rest of the family followed her. I waved them back.

"No. Please. Only Tonie. My father says Lupe needs quiet."

I brought Tonie to him.

"Do you speak English?" he asked.

She ducked her head shyly.

"Yes, sir."

"Good. Then tell your mother that your sister is very, very sick. That she must go to the hospital. Do I make myself clear?"

Tonie translated.

The message made Lupe's mother wail louder and rock her daughter more frantically.

"My mother wants to know what's wrong with Lupe."

My father mopped his forehead.

"Malnutrition," he said. "That means she doesn't eat enough or doesn't eat the right kinds of food to keep her body working well."

When Tonie translated, the poor woman rocked her daughter furiously. She cried out one of Lupe's favorite laments, *"Madre mía!"* A gush of Spanish followed.

"My mother says she knows Lupe doesn't eat enough. Each day my mother tells her, 'Eat! Eat!' But Lupe won't eat. She's afraid of getting fat."

Tonie listened to another flood of Spanish.

"My mother also says not eating is no reason for Lupe to go to the hospital. Hospitals are dirty, bad places that make you sicker. That's what my mother says. She says she'll take Lupe home and make her eat."

The woman continued talking faster than Tonie could translate. My father shook his head and tried to interrupt.

"Listen. You must listen, *señora*. Young lady, tell your mother she must understand what I am saying."

Tonie talked to her mother and shook her by the shoulders until she finally quieted a little. My father stooped down and talked directly into the woman's face.

"I'm afraid this child's sickness is no longer a simple matter of not eating because she doesn't want to get fat. At first, it may have been that, but now she can't eat. She isn't able to eat. Do you understand?"

After Tonie translated, the mother gushed more

Spanish, but Tonie hushed her. My father continued.

"She has a sickness of both the mind and the body. Doctors call it *anorexia nervosa*. She's afraid to eat food and if she does manage to get some down, she probably vomits most of it."

Guiltily, I remembered the night I found Lupe throwing up. I should have told somebody then.

Before Tonie finished translating, the woman screamed something at my father.

"My mother, she says, if you think Lupe's crazy, you're crazy. She says it's—"

The girl hesitated.

"Yes?" my father asked.

"My mother thinks it's *el mal de ojo*, the evil eye."

Sighing, my father stood up.

"These folk superstitions," he muttered.

He mopped his forehead.

"Let me put it this way, if she is to get well, she must go to a hospital. Besides special feeding, she needs counseling to get over her fear of eating."

While Tonie translated, I shook my head. I should have told somebody that I found Lupe vomiting. I should have told my father. Only I promised her I wouldn't. Besides, wasn't I afraid he would blame it all on dancing?

But now he said she needed to go to the hospital. Maybe fear wasn't her mother's only reason for saying no to that.

"Maybe they don't have enough money for a hospital," I said to my father. He shook his head impatiently.

"That can be managed. There are various health plans the family probably qualifies for. Also there's the county hospital."

On the floor, the woman wagged her head from side to side.

"No hospital! No hospital!" she cried.

Tonie looked at my father apologetically.

"I'm sorry, Doctor, but my mother says she's going to take Lupe home now."

The woman struggled to stand with Lupe in her arms. Shrugging, my father helped her and opened the door.

"They'll probably call in the nearest *curandero*," he muttered.

"What's that?" I asked.

"A healer. An old woman or man who uses herbs and magic to try to cure people."

"But that won't help her!" I cried.

He sighed.

"At first, it might have. But now, her condition is so poor..."

Joyce rushed to the door after Lupe and her mother.

"Dr. Adams, you're not going to let them take her!" Joyce cried.

"I have no choice."

Lupe opened her eyes.

"I'll be fine," she whispered.

After they left, we looked at each other silently.

"Will she die?" I asked.

My father shrugged.

"I don't know. Why couldn't I make them understand?"

His face looked tired and sad, and his usually straight shoulders sagged. He really seemed to care that Lupe was sick and he couldn't help her. I watched him leave.

"Maybe she'll be all right, Father," I called after him.

McMichael boomed into the room, almost running into my father.

"What in the name of heaven are you two girls standing around for?" he demanded of Joyce and me. "I explained about Lupe to the Adjudicator. He's an understanding man, but he came to see a ballet. So let's put one on for him."

Joyce stared at McMichael.

"But how? We've no Sleeping Beauty!"

"You know the role, Joyce," he said. "You created it."

Joyce snorted.

"You're kidding, of course. You know how awful my technique is. No way could I do all those beats I gave poor little Lupe."

McMichael cleared his throat.

"True. But Maggie here can," he said.

Joyce eyed me and her face brightened. I backed away from her.

"Oh, no," I moaned.

She caught hold of my shoulder.

"You can, Mag, and you will."

Chapter Fourteen

I didn't think I could dance the role of Sleeping Beauty, but Joyce did—or said she did.

In the dressing room, her gray eyes stared into mine. She was trying to give me some of her courage, I guess.

"For two months you've been watching Lupe," she said. "You learn steps easily. You know the role, Mag!"

McMichael rushed out to the corridor to call Ida. In seconds she had me out of the Swan Queen costume and into a blue tutu we used for the Dancing Doll in *Nutcracker*. Lupe's costume, of course, was too small.

"The blue's a trifle too dark, my darling, but the fit is good," Ida said. She took a needle and thread from the pincushion on her wrist and sewed me into the costume.

Joyce brought in Libbie, a tall, slender girl from

the corps, and zipped her into my Swan Queen costume.

"It's short and a little tight," Joyce told Ida. "Can you let out those darts? And, Libbie, don't look so hysterical. The Swan Queen only has to do a few *arabesques* and *penchés*. You're tall and do them gorgeously. Fake the steps if you can't remember them."

Joyce put on Libbie's pale yellow tutu. It was too long, because Libbie was so tall—too tall for a ballet dancer. Joyce started warming up. Suddenly, in the middle of a *plié*, she clutched my arm.

"Oh, Mag, you do think we can do it, don't you?" she asked, sounding as scared as I felt.

I pushed at my hair. This audience expected more than a good show. The Adjudicator, a famous teacher and former dancer, would notice every mistake, every weakness.

I sighed, trying to remember the number of *brisés* in Lupe's laughing, flying entrance. Instead, I remembered Lupe herself, wilted on the cold dressing room floor.

"We'll get through it," I said. "Somehow. We have to. Your ballet's got to go to the Festival. So that Lupe can dance in it there. I promised her."

Joyce hugged me.

"Good old Mag! Libbie and I'll do the best we can, won't we, Lib? And maybe the high and mighty Adjudicator will take pity on us tonight. Come on, let's go do it for Lupe's sake."

Next thing I knew, the tape recorder was playing Tchaikovsky's *Sleeping Beauty Waltz*, and I went flying into the glare of the overhead gels and the spots. I'm sure I didn't do the correct number of

94

brisés, but I filled in with *glissades* and *cabrioles* and *jetés.* I tried to be Lupe's laughing, childish Sleeping Beauty.

Near the end of the ballet, when the judge-turned-Prince Charming awarded me the golden toe shoes, I felt my summer wind stirring.

Afterwards, Joyce, of all people, was crying. She hugged me.

"Mag, you were beautiful!"

McMichael nodded. "Lupe couldn't have been a more charming Sleeping Beauty, my dear."

Mama was there, too, hugging me.

"Lovely! Lovely! I nearly cried!"

Even my father, square and towering, almost complimented me.

"You certainly were stronger than that poor malnourished little girl could have been!"

After my father, came the Adjudicator. He turned out to be lean, middle-aged, and hawk-nosed. His goatee wobbled when he smiled.

"Brilliant interpretation," he told me. "And light, clean technique."

He turned to Joyce and shook her hand.

"A very amusing idea, young lady. And you had some good coaching on the choreography. Some of the dancing seemed a little tentative, but under the circumstances tonight..."

Joyce smiled.

"Thank you very much, but what's the verdict? Do we stage it at the Festival?"

He laughed, wobbling his goatee.

"I'm afraid you'll have to wait a few weeks to find out. Before I can reach a final decision, I must view the works of several more regional companies. But

95

I'm happy to learn that all of you will be attending the Festival and taking the master classes. Ian tells me your Auxiliary raised money with bake sales to pay the tuitions of all the company members."

Joyce nodded impatiently.

"But when will we know if the ballet goes too?"

"I'll write you soon," he said. "And I shouldn't be surprised if several of your talented cast won scholarships at the Festival."

That's all he would say, but we hoped his comments would cheer Lupe when we went to see her the next afternoon. Looking for the number of her apartment, Joyce drove her mother's car around and around a dozen barrack-like buildings on the other side of town from my house. At last we found Lupe's place. Tonie opened the door and asked us into what seemed to be a combined livingroom, diningroom, and kitchen.

Alone at a table, a young man of about twenty-four mopped up beans from his plate with a folded tortilla. Beneath his thin mustache he smiled when Tonie introduced him as Manuel, her oldest brother.

"Excuse me for continuing to eat," he said, "but I have to go to work in a few minutes."

Tonie laughed nervously.

"Everybody in our crazy family works different shifts. Manuel works swing, and one of my sisters works graveyard. This week my father is working days. Our mother doesn't work, but she's babysitting over at one of my aunt's."

Tonie led us to a sofa where Lupe lay. Only her small thin face showed above a bright patchwork quilt. Her eyes were closed although the TV was on.

"She's sleeping," Tonie said. "All she's done since we brought her home is sleep."

Joyce and I looked at Lupe. Her face seemed like that of an old, old woman.

Tonie reached out to wake Lupe, but Joyce shook her head.

"Don't wake her. She needs to rest. Has she eaten anything?"

"Only a little herb broth the *curandero* mixed." I frowned.

"I don't think that's enough. Can't you talk your mother into taking her to the hospital?"

Tonie rubbed one bare foot across the other.

"My mother's against hospitals," she said. "Down where she and my father come from, the hospital is crowded and dirty."

Joyce sighed.

"What about your father? Does he believe hospitals are bad, too?"

Tonie nodded.

"He thinks the same as my mother."

Joyce shook her head. I knew how she felt. It seemed so hopeless. I looked back at Lupe's little face.

"Talk to your mother, Tonie," I said. "The hospitals aren't like that here."

Joyce turned to the grownup brother.

"Did you know that Lupe's very sick and should be in a hospital?"

I didn't know how Joyce dared speak to him. He looked like his father and seemed even more grownup and serious. He stared at her for a moment. Then he smiled beneath his thin mustache.

"My mother said Lupe just needs good food and the help of the *curandero*. She did say that some crazy Anglo doctor wanted to take Lupe to the hospital."

I felt my face burn.

"That doctor happened to be my father. He doesn't want Lupe to die!"

His eyes widened and he stopped smiling.

"Is she that sick?" he asked.

I nodded.

"My father says she has almost starved herself to death."

Wiping his mouth and fingers on a paper napkin, the brother stood up.

"I know you are good friends of Lupe and want her to get well," he said, leading Joyce and me to the door. "When she wakes up, Tonie will say you were here."

He shook hands with us.

"Thank you for coming. I have been in the hospital here. A machine where I work crushed my foot, and the ambulance took me there. Sometimes I do not believe the *curanderos* can help. I will talk to my mother."

Chapter Fifteen

That night the first rehearsal for our spring season ran late, so it was almost 10:00 P.M. when Mama brought me home. Fortunately, my father had not yet arrived.

"Some emergency must be keeping him," Mama said, putting the casserole in the microwave oven.

While I took a shower, she put my ballet clothes in the washer-dryer and set the table. She was lighting the candles when my father drove up.

"Perfect timing, for once," she said, giving a little laugh. "He'll be happy to have his family waiting for him. And, Maggie, see if you can smooth down your hair. The shower really made it bush out and wave."

My father came in the back door, kissed Mama, and glanced at me.

"I saw your little friend, the one whose part you danced last night, Maggie."

I rushed to him.

"Lupe! How is she? What happened?"

My father washed his hands at the kitchen sink and dried them on the towel Mama handed him.

"Just as I was leaving the office, Betty called me back to take a telephone call. She said the man sounded anxious. He had a slight foreign accent, she said, and was a friend of my daughter."

"So what happened?" I asked.

"It was your friend's older brother. He had overruled both his parents and stayed home from work this evening to see that she got to the hospital."

I hugged my father.

"What a relief! Joyce and I talked to him this afternoon. She'll be so glad!"

My father nodded.

"So that's where I've been. At the hospital with her whole family. But the brother took charge. He made them remain in the waiting room. Except for the mother, of course. Nobody could keep her away from her little daughter. And you'll be glad to know that your friend's father has medical coverage where he works."

"So Lupe'll be okay?" I asked. "She'll get well and be able to dance again?"

My father thrust his hands into his pockets and paced across the kitchen.

"Right now, I can't even say that she'll get well. As for dancing..." He shook his head.

"Can't you think of anything but dancing? Her condition is extremely critical, Maggie!"

I bit my lip.

"I'm sorry, Father. I thought that if she went to the hospital..."

My father laid his big hand on my wrist. For the first time since I was a little girl, since before my ballet came between us, I noticed the red hairs curling on the backs of his thick fingers.

"We'll do everything we can, Maggie."

As soon as we finished dinner, I phoned Joyce.

"Can we visit Lupe?" Joyce asked.

My father said, "Not yet."

For several weeks he continued saying the same thing every time I asked him.

And, to my nightly question, "How is she?", he replied, "About the same," when he was in a good mood. When he wasn't, he answered impatiently, "There's no change. What do you expect—miracles?"

Often several days passed without my asking him at all, because he went to bed before I got home from rehearsals. They lasted later and later, the closer we came to our spring season.

Besides the two ballets our company performed last year, we were staging *Golden Shoes*. The ballet needed a lot of work because Joyce kept changing the choreography and because Libbie and I were learning new roles.

One Saturday afternoon in the middle of a rehearsal, McMichael rushed into the classroom waving a long sheet of white paper.

"It's here! The mailman just brought it," he yelled, crackling the paper. "The Adjudication letter has come. You'll never believe what it says."

Except for Joyce, we all gathered around him. Even Cynthia.

"Did we make it? Did we make it?"

Joyce stood in the center of the room, one hand to her mouth. McMichael crackled the paper at her.

"Don't you want to know what it says?" he teased her. "Aren't you interested, Madame Choreographer?"

She asked, "Well, did we make it?"

He ambled toward her.

"Make it, my dear? Well, I'm sorry, but your ballet was simply too good for the Chamber Concert. But ask me about the Gala. Just ask me about the Gala!"

Around him, we all screamed.

"The Gala! The Gala!"

Now Joyce was screaming with the rest of us. Snatching the letter, she scanned it.

"We did," she yelled. "We were so good we made the Gala. We'll have the honor of being one of the few companies to perform at the Festival's public performance."

She threw her arms around me and, joined by the others, we waltzed hysterically around and around the classroom. We cried, "We made it! We made it!", until a sort of chant emerged:

"From the start we couldn't lose,
because we're dancing *Golden Shoes*."

Even Cynthia tossed her blond mane and danced with us. But later I heard her tell Libbie, "My ballet would have made the Gala, too."

Chapter Sixteen

As soon as my father said Lupe could have visitors, Joyce and I went to the hospital to show her the Adjudicator's letter.

Propped high on white pillows, she smiled when we entered her flower- and doll-filled room. My father said that every day her family brought more presents.

We rushed to hug her.

"We've got terrific news for you, Lupe!" Joyce said, unfolding a Xerox copy of the Adjudication letter.

I nodded. "Guess what it says!"

Lupe hardly looked at the letter. Instead, she patted the pink and lavender kerchief that hid all her hair.

"Does this scarf look funny?" she asked. Her eyes seemed darker and larger than I remembered.

"Funny?" I asked. "I don't see anything funny about it. I've seen you wear kerchiefs plenty of times."

"But before, my hair showed," she said. "It hung down below my scarves."

She stared at me with large, frightened eyes.

"Didn't your father tell you what happened to my hair?"

I shook my head. She clutched both hands to her temples.

"*Por dios*, it fell out. All of it. Because of this sickness, I'm bald."

Tears slid down her cheeks. On either side of the bed, Joyce and I patted her thin, gray-looking arms sticking out of her hospital gown.

"It'll grow back, Lupe, honey," Joyce said. "I've been reading about *anorexia*. Quite often the hair falls out. But it grows back."

I nodded.

"I'm sure it'll be as thick and shiny as ever. I'll ask my father."

But her tears continued.

"I already asked him. The other doctors too. They all say it will grow again. But how can I be sure?"

Joyce and I glanced at each other. Poor Lupe still seemed very tired and sick. My father said we shouldn't stay long. I took the letter from Joyce.

"Lupe, before we go, we want to show you the letter from the Adjudicator. Guess what it says?"

She stared at me. Her dark eyes glistened with tears. She didn't seem to understand what we were talking about.

"Lupe, do you remember that we danced Joyce's ballet for the Adjudicator?"

She nodded, continuing to finger her scarf. I glanced at Joyce, who shrugged.

"Go ahead, tell her about his letter."

"Well," I said, "he accepted Joyce's ballet for the

104

Gala. That means we'll perform it for an outside audience, not just other students at the Festival. It'll let our kids be seen by more people and give us a better chance at the scholarships various schools and companies are awarding to talented dancers."

Again Lupe only nodded. As if she didn't care. Or didn't remember *Golden Shoes*, the Adjudication, or even the Festival. I tried once more.

"The letter also praises Joyce's choreography. 'Precocious and fresh,' the Adjudicator calls it."

"That's nice," Lupe said, patting her scarf. She still didn't seem the least bit interested.

Joyce took the letter.

"It also praises Maggie's technique and interpretation of Sleeping Beauty's innocence. And did you notice, Mag, there's no mention of your braces."

I shrugged. "I guess the Adjudicator was too busy to notice."

Joyce tapped me with the letter.

"That's my point, Mag, he didn't notice and neither does anybody else."

"Well, I notice!"

Joyce studied the letter.

"Of course, it also criticizes the unevenness in the technical difficulty of the three variations."

"Which is stupid," I said. "Didn't he realize you fit the difficulty to our different technical levels?"

Joyce sighed.

"I had to do it that way. Cynthia couldn't have danced Sugarplum the way I originally choreographed it for you, Mag. But his comments about drawn-out entrances and the abruptness of the finale are valid. And I'm changing them."

Joyce dropped the letter on the bed and walked to the window, frowning. I could see that she was mentally changing the choreography. Again.

"Maybe if I had Sleeping Beauty and Prince Charming and the two boys dance forward, while Sugarplum and the Swan Queen circle with the corps..."

The crackle of paper interrupted Joyce. Lupe's thin hand lay on the letter. On the white paper it looked like a bird's claw.

"We shouldn't have stayed so long, Lupe," I said. "My father says you need lots of rest. But we wanted to tell you *Golden Shoes* will be in the Gala."

Her dark gaze met mine.

"Golden Shoes?" she asked.

I stared. "Don't you remember Joyce's ballet?"

A thin film, that seemed to have dulled her eyes, slid away.

"Oh, yes. I was going to dance the role of Sleeping Beauty, wasn't I? Before I got sick."

I squeezed her hand.

"That's right, Lupe. And when you're well again, you will dance it."

Joyce took Lupe's other hand.

"Sure you will, honey," she said. "We hope you'll dance it at the Festival."

Lupe moved her dark gaze to Joyce.

"No. But maybe my hair will grow back by then."

That night I asked my father if Lupe's sickness made her forget things. Important things like the Regional Festival and the names of ballets.

My father nodded thoughtfully.

"Her whole body is affected by the malnutrition: brain, glands, muscles, everything. So maybe she will be forgetful for a while. Please remember however, that, strange as it may seem to you, the Festival and even ballet itself are far less important to Lupe now than having her hair grow back."

Chapter Seventeen

We danced *Golden Shoes* in the spring performances without Lupe. She didn't even leave the hospital until after school let out the week before the Festival.

The day we left for the Festival, Joyce and I debated whether to visit Lupe.

"The way I see it, is this," Joyce said. "Seeing us this afternoon would remind her of all she's missing. Which might upset her. And, if it didn't upset her, it would upset us to find her so changed."

We went to the doughnut shop instead. The minute we entered, however, I wished we had gone to see Lupe. At one of the little tables sat Doug with that girl I'd seen him with at school.

My face burned and must have turned scarlet.

"What's wrong, Mag?" Joyce asked.

I stared at the trays filled with doughnuts, in the glass case.

"Nothing."

But I couldn't fool Joyce. Her glance roved over the shop and settled on Doug.

"Hum," she said. "I see a tall, gorgeous boy whose face is as red as yours. He must be the 'Doug' you've mentioned."

I continued to study the doughnuts.

"I'm not hungry, after all," I said. "Let's get out of here."

She shook her head.

"No way. I'm hungry. Besides, I think Doug's cute."

I pushed at my hair.

"But with him here, I can't stay. Especially when he's with that girl."

"Play it cool, Mag," Joyce advised. "We'll get our doughnuts. And on our way to a table, you smile sweetly at him."

My face grew hotter.

"I couldn't!"

"Sure, you could. You could even stop and say 'hi'—if you were really cool."

"Well, I'm not!"

Joyce laughed. She pointed to a lemon-filled doughnut.

"One of those, please," she told the counter girl. "And Mag wants a raspberry one."

I shook back my hair.

"I won't be able to swallow it," I said.

While the girl put our doughnuts on plates, a hand touched my shoulder. I whirled and looked up into Doug's face. Joyce was right. His face was red—as red as his t-shirt.

"I saw you come in, Mag," he said, twisting his hands behind him. "I wanted to say, 'hi.'"

The tall pretty girl remained at their table. I swallowed hard.

"Hi!" I said.

"Hi!" he repeated, laughing. "I haven't seen you since way before school was out and then only from a distance. How's your summer going so far?"

I nodded. Too vigorously.

"Okay. Pretty good. How about yours?"

"Fine. I suppose you're doing as much dancing as ever."

I nodded and looked frantically around for Joyce. She was carrying our doughnuts to a table.

"I'm with my friend. Oh, this is Joyce. Joyce, this is Doug."

She observed him slowly.

"Hi, Doug. Nice to meet you."

She turned away.

"I'll take our doughnuts to the table by the window, Mag."

I started after her, but Doug touched my arm.

"Wait a minute, Mag. I read about you being in some ballet. *Sleeping Beauty*, I think. The review said you're very talented. That's great, Mag!"

I could tell he meant it.

"Thanks. That must have been a review of the spring performances."

He nodded.

"Yeah, that was it. I'd really like to see you dance sometime."

"You almost did last Christmas," I said, laughing. Now I could laugh about almost dancing Sugarplum. He nodded.

"That was too bad. Are you in some ballet I could see now?"

I shook my head.

"No, the season's over."

"Sorry about that, but in the meantime, maybe we can get together."

"Well, tonight I'm leaving for the Regional Ballet Festival."

"More ballet, huh? How long does that last?"

"Not long. Only a few days."

I started to say I'd like to see him when I got back, but the tall girl arrived at his side. She claimed him by looping her arms around one of his.

Not even looking at me, she simpered up at him.

"Come on, Doug. We'll be late for the swim party."

He nodded.

"Sure, Marlene. In a minute. Mag, do you know Marlene?"

We nodded to each other.

"Oh, you're the ballet dancer."

Doug cleared his throat.

"Well, have a good summer, Mag. And a great time at that Festival."

After I joined Joyce by the window, I watched Doug and the girl stroll down the street. Her arms still twined around one of his.

"Look at that," I said. "She acts like she owns him."

Joyce laughed.

"Don't worry, Mag. That'll get her absolutely nowhere. It's you he likes. If you ever have time for him."

Chapter Eighteen

That evening, just as Mama and I left the house to drive to the ballet school, up drove my father.

"Where are you rushing off to?" he called, leaning out of his car window.

I sighed impatiently. He never remembered anything!

"Father, the company's leaving for the Festival at 8:30. I have to hurry."

Mama got out of her car to talk to him.

"Can you warm up your dinner, Will? Or you could wait until I get back. I won't be long."

"That's all right," he said. "I'll fix myself a drink and wait for you, Elizabeth. Have a good time, Maggie."

I couldn't believe it! Maybe he had forgotten I was going to be away from home, from my family, three whole days! Something super must have happened at the hospital, to put him in such a good mood!

"Thanks, Father."

When Mama and I arrived at the ballet school, the bus our company had chartered sat puffing in the driveway. In its lighted interior the kids were settling into their seats. Parents and friends hovered about. I kissed Mama good-bye, grabbed my suitcase and ballet bag, and scrambled out of the car and onto the bus. Everybody started yelling.

"Here's Maggie. Now we can leave!"

"Hey, Mag," Joyce called. "I saved you a seat."

I edged past the parents who still filled the aisles. "Excuse me. Excuse me."

"All ashore that's going ashore," the bus driver yelled.

I found Joyce stretched across a double seat. She had saved the one in front of her for me by piling her suitcase and ballet bag on it.

"McMichael says we each get a seat to ourselves," she said. "That way we can rest and be ready for Leonide Davidman's master class tomorrow afternoon. At least, that's what McMichael thinks!"

After we stowed our luggage under our seats, I looked around me at the confusion. Mothers and fathers, sisters and brothers, and a few boyfriends, hugged and kissed the dancers good-bye. But I missed two important people.

"Where are the Bellermonts?" I asked. "I thought Mrs. B. was one of the chaperons."

Joyce snorted.

"There was a last minute change of plans. After paying our tuitions, the Auxiliary didn't have enough money left to fly us. But Mommy bought airline tickets. She wants Cynthia to be rested for

Davidman's class tomorrow afternoon. And show up the rest of us."

I sniffed. "Wouldn't you know it?"

Then I sighed. "I really hope I'm not too tired."

Joyce shrugged.

"I doubt that flying will make much difference in Cyn's dancing. Or that a bus ride will make mine any worse. Sometimes I wonder why I don't quit."

"Don't be silly!" I brushed aside her remark, but, of course, her body was too compact for ballet, and her technique wasn't good enough.

"So who's chaperoning, if not Mrs. Bellermont?" I asked.

Joyce waved toward the front of the bus.

"McMichael's up there with Libbie's mother. And, at the last minute he got Ida to come."

"Good old Ida!" I said. "I wish Mama could come along. But she had to rush right home to give my father his dinner. She couldn't even get out of the car to see me off."

Joyce shrugged and looked out the window. I felt awful, because, of course, Joyce's mother couldn't see her off either. Her mother worked nights.

Suddenly, Joyce pointed outside.

"If your mother couldn't stay, who's that woman out there waving at you?"

Mama! It was my mother! In spite of letting warm air into the air-conditioned bus, I shoved open the window and reached out to hug her.

"Goodbye, baby," she said, kissing me. "Have a wonderful time."

Hugging her back, I suddenly felt sad about leaving her. I started to cry.

113

"Oh, Mama! Come with me."

She shook her head.

"You know I can't, but don't cry, Maggie. Things are starting to work out at home. You have a good time."

I clung to her until the bus driver shouted at me to shut the damned window. Mama peeled my arms from around her neck. Joyce lowered the window and gave me a Kleenex. The bus backed out of the driveway.

In spite of McMichael's good intentions, we didn't get much sleep. Chattering and eating cookies, the girls in front of me got carsick. They had to vomit into the long paper cups the bus company provided in the pockets on the backs of chairs.

"What a bunch of infants!" Joyce said.

During the first part of the long night, Ida, McMichael, and Libbie's mother lurched up and down the aisle, trying to quiet the chatter and the singing. Everybody except me seemed to know the song about a lonely bird singing in a tree.

"How come you don't know 'Kookaburra,' Mag?" Joyce asked. "Didn't you sing it in Girl Scouts?"

I shook my head.

"I didn't have time for Girl Scouts. I always had ballet lessons."

Later, when the towns grew blacker and more deserted, our chaperons tried to get some sleep themselves. I finally dozed off and don't remember anything from the time I saw the sky paling behind the steep, dark mountain range, until the bus stopped at the hotel.

Our company scrambled out of the bus and into the red-carpeted lobby. It was already filled with shrill-voiced young dancers.

McMichael registered us, gave us identification badges, Festival programs, room keys, and instructions.

"The hotel's so crowded we have to sleep four-to-a-room," he said. "That means three dancers and one chaperon to a room. Now, remember, your behavior reflects on me and our company. So behave yourselves."

We started to dart away, but Ida motioned us back.

"Just a little advice from an old lady, my darlings. Rest today. Be quiet today. Later, there is time for excitement. Now find your rooms, take warm showers, eat good breakfasts, then return to your rooms for naps."

She had more to say, but we were too excited to listen. Comparing keys, Joyce and I discovered that we were roommates. We hugged each other and dashed to the elevator. Our room was on the third floor—315.

Rushing along the third floor corridor, we read the numbers aloud as we passed each door.

"312, 313, 314. Here it is—315."

When Joyce turned her key in the lock, the knob twisted but the door would not open. She tried again and I tried, but neither of us succeeded.

"It's bolted on the inside," she said. "Somebody got here before us."

We stared at each other.

"Oh, no!" I cried. "The Bellermonts! They got here last night on the plane."

At that moment a lock clicked. We stepped back just as the door swung open. In the entrance stood Mrs. Bellermont in a long, flowered polyester robe. Her hairdo was under repair on rollers nearly the size of sewer pipes.

From a bed behind Mrs. Bellermont rose a head curtained with long hair. A hand pushed aside the blond drape to reveal Cynthia Bellermont's plump, sleepy face.

"Who is it, Mommy?"

"Them!" Mrs. Bellermont replied. "Looking like things the cat dragged in. And in simply lovely shape for Leonide Davidman's class this afternoon."

Chapter Nineteen

After large breakfasts, short naps, and no lunch, Joyce and I made it to Davidman's master class. But we heard an awful rumor when we finally squeezed into the diningroom, where portable ballet *barres* and a hundred ballet students replaced the usual tables and chairs. At the last minute, Davidman could not leave New York.

"And guess who's replacing him?" buzzed the girl next to me at the barre. "That dreamy Larry Randall. Isn't that terrific?"

I didn't think so. I clutched Joyce's arm.

"If that's true, I'm getting out of here. Randall hates me."

"Don't worry, Mag. Even if he is here, he won't notice you in this crowd."

I looked along the *barres*. Joyce was right. I was just another student in pink toe shoes, pink tights, and black leotard. At least half of them wore braces on their teeth. Several even had red hair. Everybody looked so much alike that for a moment I didn't even recognize Cynthia bouncing up to us.

"You two barely made it," she said. "Mommy brought me down early so I could get a good place at the *barre*. Libbie's saving it for me now. Mommy's out talking to Larry Randall."

I bit my lip.

"Then it's true. Randall is replacing Davidman."

"Oh, yes. Mommy's out there reminding him about me."

She turned away sighing.

"Only I wish she wouldn't. Even if he is goodlooking, he scares me. After *barre* work, I'm going to hide in the back row of dancers."

"Poor old Cyn," Joyce said.

Cynthia turned her saucer-shaped eyes on Joyce.

"You know, I'm not as good as Mommy thinks. She should have been the dancer, not me."

Tears bubbled up in Cynthia's eyes. She wiped them away with a pink hand towel she carried in case she happened to sweat—which was unlikely, since she never worked hard enough.

She grasped a lock of her long hair. Every other girl wore her hair tied back in a ponytail or bun, but Cynthia's flowed loose.

"And look at my hair. Mommy thinks it's simply lovely like this."

Joyce laughed.

"You do look more like Rapunzel than a dancer."

"It's not funny. Mommy doesn't seem to realize that every time I move, I get hair in my teeth and eyes. Does anybody have an extra rubber band or something?"

I handed her the blue ribbon I had tied around my ponytail to make me stand out from the others. With

Randall teaching, I no longer wanted to stand out. I wanted to melt into the crowd.

Suddenly everybody hushed, and Larry Randall glided in, carrying a gold-topped stick. He wore white tights, white ballet shoes, and a tight gold t-shirt with his initials, LR, stamped over his heart. His profile remained as purely shaped as last Christmas, but he no longer wore his hair slicked down. It flowed to his shoulders in a neat blond bob.

Randall surveyed the room without really looking at anyone. He tapped his gold-topped stick on the floor.

"In my classes, ladies and gentlemen," he began in the stuck-up voice I remembered so well, "we will work for placement. At all times, precise movements. Precise positions. When I say fifth position, I mean fifth position."

He wedged his feet parallel. The toe of one foot pressed the heel of the other.

"I don't mean something halfway between a first and a third," he continued, gazing toward the room's high ceiling. "I mean fifth position. Precisely."

He lifted his profile and tapped his stick for emphasis.

"During my master classes, ladies and gentlemen, your time and your money—or your company's money—will be well spent if you achieve one thing, elementary though it may seem: a precise fifth!"

Next to me at the barre, Joyce snorted.

"Which he doubts any of us is talented enough to do."

The place was absolutely quiet. No one moved. No one's weight creaked the wooden *barres*. Even so, Randall must have had uncanny hearing to notice Joyce's whisper in the huge room.

119

But he did. His glance shot to her. Then to me. Where it hovered until his eyes glinted. His nostrils flared. Oh, no! He remembered me! He banged his stick.

"If the young lady with the red hair and braces will kindly stop whispering, I will demonstrate the first exercise."

Of course, everyone gawked at me. My face burned, but I sucked in my middle, wedged my feet into a tight fifth, and glared straight ahead.

Randall rapped his stick.

"Order!" he yelled. "Turn around."

When everybody faced him again, he bent his knees to show us a *plié* combination.

Only after the pianist started banging the grand piano did Joyce dare whisper again.

"Sorry, Mag!"

Unfortunately, after we finished half an hour of *barre* exercises, Randall noticed me again. He motioned us to form lines across the room and insisted that I work right in front of him.

He placed his stick to mark the spot.

"Precisely here," he said. "I want the redheaded girl where I can see her. I won't have her disrupting my class again."

A couple of times at school I've seen kids walk out when they weren't treated nearly as unfairly, but years of ballet discipline made me obey. I took a fifth position on the spot he pointed out and continued to point out each time the other dancers changed rows.

Usually, keeping a pupil in the front row shows a teacher's interest. But not with me. And not with Randall. Whenever I looked at him, his nostrils flared furiously.

Just before class ended, he showed a variation that was practically a military drill.

"I want every position, every movement precise. Please remember, precision is the key to good dancing."

When he tapped his stick, the pianist played and the dancers danced.

Suddenly, he banged his stick close to my toes. The music and dancing stopped. In the hush, Randall nodded his head toward me.

"Apparently, our redheaded young lady imagines she's a ballerina, and does not have to follow my directions. Pray, Madame Ballerina, favor us with your interpretation of my variation."

Stepping away from him, I shook my head.

"I really don't know..." I began.

"But you do! You just did. Music, please."

My face stiff and hot, I danced the variation as well as I could. When I finished, the other dancers applauded until he pounded his stick.

"That will do! Obviously, no one in this room understands what I am trying to teach. You applaud this girl who, instead of working precisely, flits and glides like a Giselle or a Sugarplum Fairy."

He strode toward the door.

"I am wasting my time here. Obviously, none of you wants to improve. And, just as obviously, not one of you will ever become a professional dancer."

After the door slammed behind him, kids crowded around me.

"Don't mind him!" they said. "You looked great. Beautiful."

"I don't know," I cried. "I just know I'm getting out of his class. I hope I never see him again."

Chapter Twenty

At dinner that night, I sat at the opposite end of the diningroom from Randall's yellow head. Later, I looked for him at the Chamber Concert, but I guess he considered those little ballets too trivial to bother with. I did see McMichael, though, when the performance was over.

"You've got to get me out of Randall's class!"

"Yes, I heard you had trouble with him this afternoon, Maggie."

"You heard? Who told you?"

"News travels fast at Festivals. Several people mentioned it. Including Mrs. Bellermont."

"So she was there!"

McMichael laughed.

"You don't think Jean Bellermont would miss a master class her daughter was taking! She watched through the glass doors and reported that you were whispering. You deserved what you got, she said. But

I think she'd give her Lincoln Continental to have Cynthia get the attention Randall gave you!"

I sighed.

"Cynthia's welcome to it. And I wasn't whispering. Would you please get me into Martina's class tomorrow?"

McMichael nodded.

"I will. But don't think too badly of Jean Bellermont, my dear. Without her and her Auxiliary, I doubt we'd have a company."

In spite of McMichael's advice, I did think badly of Mrs. Bellermont, and Randall, too, all the way up to my room. When I opened the door, however, I had to forget both of them.

"Surprise! Surprise!"

The kids in our company jumped out at me from behind doors and chairs and from among loops of crepe paper and bunches of red and blue balloons. On a bedside table, a flat white cake blazed with candles. Through the flames I read a message in red icing:

Happy 15th Birthday, Maggie Adams!

Next came the happy birthday song, lots of giggling, blowing out candles, hugging everyone. Finally, I settled crosslegged on one of the beds to open gifts ranging from lambs wool for tender toes to a shiny autographed photograph of Makarova.

I clasped the picture to my chest.

"My favorite ballerina! Who's this from?"

To my astonishment, Cynthia waggled her hand. "Me."

Before I could even thank her, Mrs. Bellermont jumped up from her chair near the window.

"Why, Cynthia Anne! How could you? I brought that picture clear back from New York. Especially for you."

On the bed across from me, Cynthia stared down at her hands while Mrs. Bellermont went on and on.

"Well, I don't think it's very nice of you to give it away. I went to a great deal of trouble to get the photograph signed for you. Why are you giving it to Maggie?"

"It's her birthday."

"Well, I think Maggie should return it. You shouldn't have given it away."

I handed the photograph across to Cynthia reluctantly because I really wanted it.

"Thanks, Cyn, but I guess your mother's right."

"She's not! She's not!"

Cynthia snatched her hands behind her back and would not take the photograph. In the now silent room she glared at her mother.

"Didn't you give it to me?"

"Of course, Cynthia Anne, that's why I'm so upset."

"Then it's mine, isn't it?"

"Yes. That's what I'm saying. It was a gift from me, your mother."

"Then it's my property and I can give it to Maggie."

Smoothing down her long skirt, Mrs. Bellermont sank back on her chair. She sighed.

"I don't know what's making Cynthia Anne so rebellious these days!"

Next morning Joyce and I attended a lecture on dieting for fat dancers, but we left early because neither of us is fat, and because dieting reminded us of poor Lupe. We went over to the empty diningroom to warm up for Martina's class.

Wearing practice clothes, Martina soon limped in.

An elastic bandage supported her left knee. The tendonitis, that took her out of our company's *Nutcracker* last Christmas, had forced her to give up dancing altogether. Now she was ballet mistress for City Ballet and taught at the company's school.

To my surprise, she remembered Joyce and me.

"Maggie, I hoped I would see you here. I noticed your name in the program. And, Joyce, you have a ballet in the Gala tonight. Congratulations! Thank you both for coming to my class."

She limped across the room to talk to the pianist. Joyce shook her head.

"Too bad she had to quit dancing! She's such a contrast to Randall!"

The class Martina taught was a contrast to his, too. Even the *barre* exercises had movement and exciting rhythms.

When we moved to the center of the floor, Martina spoke in such a soft voice that we had to strain to hear her in the large room.

"As I said yesterday, I emphasize movement. Dancing must flow. It is not a series of poses. Dancers move."

She paused.

"Unfortunately, my poor knee keeps me from moving anymore. But watch my hands. They will show you what to do and how I want you to do it."

Her slim, long-fingered hands twisted and fluttered, pantomiming the steps at the same time that she named them.

After several variations that sent us flying and spinning across the floor, I turned breathlessly to Joyce.

"This is really dancing!"

Martina's final combination was a difficult string of turning leaps and spinning *arabesques*. Although

I'm quick at learning steps, it took me a couple of run-throughs before I could do this variation well. Dancing it the last time, though, I felt my summer wind rise and lift me through the flow and rhythms of Martina's lovely combination.

After class, I pressed toward the door, blotting sweat from my neck and shoulders with my towel. I was exhausted but I also felt a purity—a happiness that comes to me when I have danced hard and well.

I heard someone call me and looked back to see Martina beckoning me to stay in the emptying room. She, too, looked tired, but her smile was quiet and beautiful. It had the purity I was feeling.

"Maggie, last Christmas I thought you were a very promising dancer. Now you're even better. You've made so much progress. And you dance with such feeling!"

My face burned with pleasure. She touched my shoulder.

"I want you to come study with me at City Ballet School."

I gasped.

"How wonderful, but..."

I stopped, thinking of my father and the objections he would make.

"I don't know," I said. "It's so far. It would take so much time. And cost a lot of money. At McMichael's I have a scholarship."

Martina shrugged.

"All those little details can be arranged, Maggie. It's not that far. And, if you dance as well in the Gala tonight as you did in class today, I'm sure City Ballet School will offer you a scholarship."

"Do you really think so?"

She nodded.

"Just keep your fingers crossed, Maggie."

Chapter Twenty-One

Maybe Martina was joking when she said, "Keep your fingers crossed," but every time I remembered during the rest of the day, I crossed them.

At lunch, Joyce moaned, "I just hope the lighting cues work tonight." I crossed my fingers. Twice, during the afternoon modern dance class, I also remembered.

In the evening, when I started to warm up for the Gala, I noticed some slick spots on the ballroom's stage. I rubbed my toe shoes in the rosin box and complained to Joyce. I also crossed my fingers.

"We'll break our necks," I said.

Joyce frowned.

"They said they wet down the floor this morning after the Chamber Concert last night, but I'll go see what I can do."

She returned with a jar of water and sprinkled the slippery spots.

"Get that one too," I said, pointing to a shiny area near the center.

Joyce tried, but a few minutes later I landed there from a flying series of *brisés*. My left foot slipped, twisted, and wrenched. Pain shot from my ankle up my whole left leg. I collapsed on the floor.

"It's my ankle," I moaned to McMichael and the dancers crowding around me.

"Can you stand on it?" McMichael asked, helping me up. Cautiously, I shifted part of my weight to my left foot. I groaned.

"I can't. It hurts too much."

I started to cry. I wished my father were there to take care of me.

McMichael examined my foot.

"It's starting to swell," he said. "We'll have to get you to a hospital."

I struggled away from him, hopping on my good foot.

"I can't go," I cried. "I can't let Joyce down."

I bit my lip. Besides, there was the scholarship Martina mentioned. I had to dance in the Gala in order to win the scholarship.

Looking around, I saw Joyce standing alone in the wings. Her face looked frozen. I hopped toward her.

"I'll be all right, Joyce. It's just a kink that I'll work out with a few exercises. Like in class last year."

Joyce looked at me. She put out an arm to steady me.

"Don't be stupid, Mag. You've got to go to the hospital. Your ankle could be sprained. Even broken."

I clutched her arm.

"But what about your ballet? Who'll dance Sleeping Beauty if I don't?"

She sighed.

"Well, maybe you will. Depending on what they say at the hospital. Maybe you'll be back in time. *Golden Shoes* is next-to-last on the program."

I nodded.

"I'm sure it's only a little twist."

Once more I tried to put my weight on it. Bright, hot pain flamed up to my hip. I groaned.

Joyce shook her head.

"I don't think so, Mag."

"Then who'll dance Sleeping Beauty?" I cried, "With me and Lupe gone?"

Joyce lifted her chin.

"I will. I'll have to. I'll get Stephanie to replace me in the corps."

The mother of a member of the local regional company that was hosting the Festival drove me to the hospital. Libbie's mother, one of our chaperons, wrapped me in my shawl and came along.

"It's nice of you to come," I said, wishing my father were there instead.

We followed the red signs to the emergency entrance of the hospital, and stopped beside the ramp. Before Libbie's mother could open the car door, an orderly and a nurse did it for her. They helped me into an examining room and onto a table. The intern on duty looked about Joyce's age, but his long slim hands swiftly and carefully removed my left toe shoe, and probed my swollen ankle.

"Hmm, another dancer," he said, smiling. "From the Festival? You're the third this weekend. Dancing must be almost as dangerous as skiing. The ankle looks sprained, but we'll send you to Xray to make sure."

He helped the nurse slide me into a wheelchair

131

which she pushed to the white, concrete cave, where a technician made an X-ray. It confirmed that my ankle was not broken.

Back in the examining room, the intern wound an ace bandage from my heel to lower calf.

"What about dancing?" I asked him. "Since it's only sprained, can I dance tonight? It's really important."

He shook his head.

"No way! It's a fairly bad sprain and I want you in a wheelchair until the swelling goes down. Then on crutches for about a week. And no dancing for four to six weeks. Then you'd better check with your own doctor."

"My father's a doctor," I said, thinking maybe if I called him, he'd say it was okay to dance tonight. Only I knew he wouldn't.

The intern smiled.

"Then you'll be in good hands."

I nodded and sighed. Keeping my fingers crossed sure hadn't helped much. But at least my ankle wasn't broken.

When we returned to the hotel, a bellboy brought me a wheelchair, and Libbie's mother got me upstairs and into bed. The pills the intern gave me to kill the pain kept me from hearing either my roommates return from the Gala, or the Bellermonts leaving for breakfast the next morning.

When I did wake up, I first felt the pain of my ankle, and then I noticed the clock on my bedside table. Ten o'clock. I had missed breakfast, and I was starving.

To my surprise, Joyce still sprawled in the next bed. One arm covered her eyes. It was unlike Joyce to skip a meal.

"How come you're missing breakfast?" I asked.

She raised herself on one elbow.

"I'm not hungry. How's the ankle?"

"Painful. How was your ballet?"

Joyce snorted.

"The same."

"It couldn't have been that bad!"

"It was. I plodded through Sleeping Beauty with my usual lead feet. You know, I've got no *ballon*, and I created that whole role on Lupe's lightness, and then on yours. It was a disaster."

Joyce lay back and stared at the ceiling. I had never seen her so discouraged.

"What about the other kids?" I asked.

"They went to pieces. Cyn was as awful as ever. Libbie missed a cue and lost her cool. I thought Stephanie would be able to follow the rest of the corps. Instead, she threw the others off. Only the boys had enough experience to pull off their roles fairly smoothly."

I shook my head.

"I'm so sorry, Joyce. But I'm sure it's not as bad as you think."

"Worse, probably."

Moving carefully to avoid hurting my ankle, I sat up.

"Tell you what, Joyce, you help me into that wheelchair, and we'll go downstairs and find some breakfast. Things always look better after you eat."

Joyce shook her head.

"I spent most of the night thinking. And I've made up my mind. I'm quitting ballet."

"Don't be ridiculous. You're a good choreographer. We just had bad luck last night."

She nodded.

"We sure did. But I've known for a long time that I'm an awful dancer. And you know there's no shortage of amateur choreographers."

"You'll change your mind."

"No, this disaster was just the last straw. I didn't tell you, but I applied and was accepted to the university."

I lowered my feet over the edge of the bed. My ankle began to throb. I pushed at my tangled hair.

"Wait until the banquet tonight, Joyce. I'm sure you'll receive some kind of award for your ballet."

And she did.

Near the end of the list of honors and awards given out by the Regional Association, the association president mentioned *Golden Shoes*:

"Despite an uneven performance, *Golden Shoes*, the only ballet choreographed by a student, shows enormous humor and talent. And since our Festival is a showcase to display and encourage talent, it is my pleasure to award Joyce Mallory a certificate of merit."

Seated in my wheelchair, I clutched one of Joyce's hands.

"You see? I told you so."

She gave me a tired smile.

"What does it mean? What do any of those awards mean? They're not worth money, like scholarships. It's just something for my scrapbook."

But she walked to the head table to collect her certificate. When she returned, I patted her arm.

"Congratulations."

"Thanks, Mag, but I'm going to college in September."

I kept trying.

"Then you can major in dance at the university, and develop your talent for choreography."

She smiled sadly.

"Forget it, Mag. I'll study something entirely different. Like Greek or law or something. But, listen! They're announcing the scholarship winners. You're sure to be one of them."

Now it was my turn to shake my head.

"Not after I missed dancing in the Gala. Martina said it depended on that."

Joyce shushed me.

"Be quiet. Listen!"

The president's voice droned on.

"We have a number of important scholarships to announce. And the first goes to the young lady you've seen around here today in a wheelchair."

Joyce squeezed my arm.

"Didn't I tell you?"

"We had hoped to see her dance in the Gala last night," the president continued, "but the last minute injury that put her in the wheelchair prevented her from performing. She has been so highly recommended, however, that City Ballet School is awarding her a full tuition scholarship. Wheel yourself up here, Maggie Adams!"

Chapter Twenty-Two

When our bus first bounced into the driveway of the ballet school, I didn't see Mama waiting for me on the porch. Her pale linen dress and the quiet way she stood made her blend into the twilight and in with the gathering of other parents.

"Hey, there's your mom!" Joyce said. "Do you ever have some surprises for her! Do you think she'll freak out when she sees your ankle? Maybe I should dash ahead and prepare her."

Joyce left while I waited for the rest of the tired company to ease themselves and their luggage off the bus. After the aisle cleared, Mama came to me, followed by Joyce.

"What a shame, honey!" Mama said, kissing me. "Are you in much pain?"

I was, but I didn't want to complain in front of Joyce.

"Not much," I said.

"Just lots of mental anguish," Joyce said, "but old Mag came out on top. Tell your mom about the scholarship, Mag."

I did.

"That's wonderful!" Mama cried, hugging me. Then she paused. "But your father won't like you commuting to the City, will he?"

"I'm afraid not."

I used the backs of the seats to support myself down the aisle.

At the door, McMichael and the father of one of the other dancers lifted me down the steps and into Mama's car.

"Well, take it easy, Mag," Joyce said, going off to meet her own mother. "I'll call you sometime."

I gazed after her. Already she sounded so far away, out of my life. Could she really quit ballet?

Mama opened the car door and slid onto the front seat.

"Joyce is going away to college," I said.

Mama frowned.

"That's what I'd like to do," she said, starting the engine, "and what your father wants you to do. We'll have to find a time and a way to tell him about your scholarship, won't we?"

When we arrived at the house, he was not home yet. And when he did drag in at ten o'clock after an emergency at the hospital, there was my sprained ankle to discuss. He examined it and cross-examined me. He wanted to know exactly how I fell, and precisely what the intern said. For a while, I was afraid he intended to confirm the diagnosis with a long distance telephone call to the intern.

"This is what comes of all this dancing," he said.

"It's a wonder you didn't fracture your ankle. Or your silly little neck!"

Without needing to ask Mama, I knew that now was not the time to bring up my scholarship.

For two whole weeks my father made me hobble around on crutches. He fit rubber pads to the top crossbars, but the crutches still made my underarms so sore that I stayed in one place most of the time. I read. I stared at soap operas. I listened to my stereo. My mind went stale. So did my body that was accustomed to so much exercise.

"Mama!" I screamed one afternoon. "I'm bored. If I don't get out of this house, I'll go crazy!"

She came from the kitchen, drying her hands down the front of her apron.

"Join the club," she said, shutting the drapes against the summer sun.

And in the darkened room, I watched her, so neat and slim, continue to dry her hands on her apron.

"Is it always like this around here?" I asked. "Always so boring?"

She gave a little laugh.

"Oh, I have things to do."

"Like what? Cleaning the house and getting dinner for father?"

She nodded. Her mouth curved into a gentle crescent.

"And going to Physicians' Wives Society luncheons. And washing ballet clothes."

I sat up on the sofa.

"From now on, you're not to wash a single leotard or pair of tights. I'll even sew the ribbons on my toe shoes! For gosh sakes, I'm fifteen!"

Mama laughed.

"Bravo! Maggie's growing up!"

She stopped laughing.

"But what do I do instead of washing your ballet clothes and doing charitable works with the PWS?"

I shrugged.

"What do you want to do? I want to take ballet lessons and dance, more than anything in the world. I suppose you could take ballet lessons, too."

Mama gave a short laugh.

"Wouldn't your father love that! Though he might not mind if I took them as a pastime. What he objects to is your disrupting our family by pouring your whole life into ballet."

I set both feet flat on the floor.

"Well, ballet is my life. And I've got to get back to it soon. I'm going to start walking right now, and tonight I'll tell him about my scholarship."

Mama shook her head.

"Wait for the right time, Maggie."

"That'll never come."

I took a step without my crutches. My ankle hurt only a little.

My father came home early enough that night to examine my ankle before dinner.

"It's swollen a little more than it has been, Maggie, You've been walking on it, haven't you?"

I nodded.

"It's been two weeks, Father. I'm so bored. I've got to get back on it sometime. I've got to get back to dancing."

"Back to dancing! Back to dancing! So you can sprain the other ankle?" he asked.

Mama rubbed her hands up and down her apron, but I tried to stay calm.

140

"It hardly hurt at all, Father, when I walked on it. I only went from here to my bedroom. I want to strengthen it gradually."

His hands continued to massage my ankle.

"Well, it doesn't seem much more swollen. Maybe it's time to start putting a little weight on it. But no ten-mile hikes. And no dancing."

Mama shook her head at me. She needn't have. Tonight I was satisfied with one small victory, getting off my crutches. I knew enough not to mention the scholarship.

A few evenings later, my father told me Lupe came for a checkup that afternoon.

"She seems to be doing quite well. Her hair's growing back and her skin looks smoother."

"But how does she feel about eating?" I asked. "Wasn't that one of the biggest problems?"

He nodded.

"Now her attitude about food seems more normal. Of course, she's still going to counseling. And she does seem to be gaining a little weight."

I leaned forward on the sofa.

"Did she ask about dancing? When can she start classes again?"

"Maggie! Maggie! Always the same question! When can Lupe get back to dancing? When can I?"

I shrugged.

"Well, we want to know, Lupe and I. Did she ask?"

"As a matter of fact, Maggie, she didn't. Maybe she's a little shy of me. Or afraid. So I told her, 'If you keep making such good progress, we'll soon have you dancing again. Would you like that, Lupe?'"

"And, of course, she said yes!"

He shook his head.

"She said she didn't know."

"That's because she knows how you feel about ballet!"

He sighed.

"I don't know. It may still be the listlessness caused by the malnutrition. Or, perhaps she's lost interest. But to get back to what I feel about ballet, Maggie. Just how do you think I feel about it?"

I hesitated. In the kitchen the rattle of pans stopped and I knew Mama was listening. A few months ago, or even a couple of weeks ago, I would have shouted at him, "You hate it! You hate ballet!" But now I pushed at my hair and told myself to play it cool.

"Well," I said carefully, "you think that I'm spending all my time on ballet at the expense of family and friends, and that there's no future for me in dancing."

He nodded.

"Yes, I do. You're cheating yourself out of a normal life. And for what? Dancing is a very short and poorly paid career. And only a talented few succeed at all."

I proceeded cautiously. I felt like a chess player. But this was no game. My life depended on my moves.

"I know it's poorly paid in money, Father. Also, unless you're like Alicia Alonzo or Fonteyn, you perform only about twenty years. But afterwards, lots of dancers go into teaching or choreography. Look at McMichael."

"This is what happens to the talented few," my father said. "Are you one of those, Maggie?"

My mother stood in the kitchen doorway. Our gazes met. She made no signal, but I felt the right

142

time was now. I hoped I was finding the right way. I took a deep breath.

"Yes, Father. I'm one of the talented. At the Festival I received a full tuition scholarship to the City Ballet School."

Chapter Twenty-Three

I waited for my father to explode after I told him about the scholarship. He didn't. But neither did he congratulate me. He leaned back, his chin on one hand, a frown between his eyes.

"When does the scholarship begin?" he asked.

"September."

"I suppose this ballet school is in the City."

"Yes."

"That means a commute of almost fifty miles each way," he said. "How many times a week?"

My glance met Mama's in the kitchen doorway. I pushed at my hair.

"Six days a week, Father."

"What are you planning to do about school? Continue, I hope."

His sarcasm stung. My face grew hot, but I kept my temper.

"It will be just like last year. I'll go to school until noon."

"Then you'll be taking only four classes at school."

"That's all I took last year."

Standing up, he stuffed his hands into his trouser pockets. He gazed out at the twilight.

"That's not enough. Or perhaps you don't consider an education important."

I wouldn't let him incite angry retorts from me this time. Pretend you're playing chess, I warned myself.

"Father, I'm taking English, social studies, Spanish, and geometry this year."

"What about typing and shorthand? Only a few ballet companies pay a living wage. If you continue dancing, you'll need a job to support yourself. I want you to take typing and shorthand."

I hesitated. I looked at Mama but she shrugged.

"I suppose I could take them in summer school."

I said it only to quiet him, to put him off, because summers I would be taking ballet classes all day, every day, at City Ballet School.

"That's a good idea," Mama said from the doorway.

My father turned to glare at her.

"I suppose you're all for this scholarship. Do you plan to drive her to these ballet classes in the city?"

She rubbed her hands down her apron.

"I don't see how I can," she said.

"Then, does Maggie intend to get an apartment in the city? Move away from the family entirely?"

My stomach clenched. Was it still last Christmas? Hadn't anything changed? He seemed so understanding about Lupe's dancing. But Lupe wasn't his daughter.

146

I jumped up and felt my ankle twinge. The pain reminded me to move slowly, both physically and with my father.

"I'll take the bus both ways," I told him. "It'll be the same as last year. Except that Mama won't have to pick me up at the ballet school."

He remained hunched against the big window.

"How will you get home from the bus depot? Walk the three miles through the dark?"

Mama dropped onto the arm of the sofa where I sat.

"I'll pick her up at the depot. It'll only take fifteen minutes."

"And you have nothing better to do than chauffeur her around."

His sarcasm hung in the air. Mama's face paled.

"I'll make the time. It gives me a chance to talk to Maggie as well as being useful. I'll also continue to do useful things like cleaning the house and getting your dinner. But from now on, daytime is my time. I've enrolled at the junior college."

"Bravo!" I said, ignoring my father's scowl.

A few days ago Mama said, "Bravo! Maggie's growing up!" I wanted to shout the same to her.

But my father glowered.

"College? What for?"

She shrugged.

"The usual reasons."

"But you're no eighteen-year-old. You're a grown woman. A wife. A mother."

"I'm a person!" she cried.

"Oh, I see. Women's Lib."

"Maybe. Why not? My husband and daughter lead fascinating lives. Why can't I?"

147

My father turned away.

"Well, as long as it doesn't interfere with things around here. But I wish it were Maggie going to college."

"Maybe she will someday," Mama said. "If and when she wants to."

But when this September came, it was Mama, as well as Joyce, who started college.

Before Joyce left, she phoned to say good-bye and wish me luck at City Ballet School.

"Just stay out of Larry Randall's path," she said, "and everything's sure to turn up roses for you."

In class things usually did turn up roses with only a few thorns. I loved the variations Martina gave, but she worked me harder and demanded more than McMichael ever had.

Some nights I could hardly drag myself to the bus depot. On the long ride home, unless there was room to stretch my legs across an adjoining seat, they ached and cramped.

Early in October, casting began for City Ballet's *Nutcracker*. All the principal roles and most of the corps parts would go to company members, but the children's dances and a few minor corps variations always went to students from the school.

One day, after a particularly hard class, Martina asked me to wait.

"I signed you up to audition for the 'Waltz of the Flowers,'" she said. "Last year you danced the Rose solo with your regional company, but with City Ballet, dancing the waltz with the corps is the very best a student can hope for."

I no longer felt tired.

"Oh, thank you, Madame. But I'm new to the

school. Do you really think I might be chosen?"
    She nodded.
    "You're new, but you're making excellent progress.
Yes, I think you'll dance in *Nutcracker*."

Chapter Twenty-Four

Auditions took place one rainy Saturday afternoon in City Ballet School's largest classroom. Lines of students wound up the staircase from the first floor, through the dim hall, and to the door of the studio.

Electric bulbs burned palely along the walls. From the skylights high above came a grayness and the constant clatter of rain. Shivering in the long line, I hugged my shawl closer and pulled up my woolen leg warmers. I did a few more *pliés*. It was hard to keep your muscles warm, waiting like this.

"It's scary the first time," said Kathy, a girl from my class. She sat cross-legged, pounding her knees on the floor to stretch her turn-out. "But you'll soon get used to auditions."

I sighed.

"Well, I'm not used to them yet. What happens?"

My new friend explained.

"Well, of course, this is just a school audition.

When you get to the door you sign in with the secretary—okay? Then you join a group of five or six to dance a combination the ballet master demonstrates. It's probably something from the *Nutcracker* that Madame Martina's been teaching us."

I nodded.

"And when do you know if you're accepted?"

"On Monday. There'll be a list on the call board. It'll have the names of the students who made it and the roles they'll dance."

I shivered. I missed McMichael's warm little ballet school. And Lupe and Joyce. I even missed Cynthia Bellermont.

When I finally reached the door of the classroom, I signed the list Kathy had mentioned. The secretary looked at my name.

"All right, Maggie. Your group's warming up at the *barre*."

I joined five girls including Kathy.

"Relax," she whispered. She pointed to the six students who were auditioning then. "See. They're dancing the 'Waltz of the Flowers.' You know it. Madame taught us."

I nodded and stared around the studio. After the cold gray corridor, the classroom seemed sunlit with its mirrors and bright fluorescent lamps.

At the judges' table in front sat the company director, two men I didn't recognize, and Martina. They studied the six performers and made notes.

When the group finished dancing, the students bowed toward the table and then toward the piano. To the pianist? I glanced over at the old upright. Against it lounged Larry Randall. The dancers were bowing to him!

My face must have paled. Kathy touched me.

"Are you sick, Maggie? Put your head between your knees. You look like you're going to faint."

I felt faint, but reminded myself that Randall was no Nagy or Baryshnikov. Only an adequate and very temperamental principal dancer.

"I'm okay," I told Kathy.

Randall, who was acting as ballet master that afternoon, dismissed the group with a rap of his cane. Ambling to the center of the room, he banged his stick again.

"Next group," he called. "And, please, young ladies, remove the leg warmers. This is not northern Siberia!"

With the others, I skinned off my knitted outer tights and hung them with my shawl over the *barre*. We lined up in front of him.

"Stand in the same order you signed in," he said, eying us.

He took a paper off the table and called our names. Mine came last.

"Maggie Adams. Which are you? Oh, yes, the redhead with braces."

He banged his cane on a spot at the end of the line.

"Over here, Maggie Adams. Didn't you hear me read the names?"

He rapped his cane again.

"Remember, young ladies, I expect tight fifth positions."

He glanced along our line.

"Of course, this year none of you will dance the variation I'm going to show. Or probably any other year, either. But I understand you learned it in class. I'll show it once. And only once. So pay attention."

He rapped his cane for the pianist to begin. Out clanged the opening phrases of the "Dance of the

153

Sugarplum Fairy." A warm shiver ran through me. Here was my variation. I must have smiled. At the front table Martina smiled back.

But, watching Randall show the variation, I grew indignant. You could tell he thought it was a corny old classic. He flapped through the steps like a lanky, blond flamingo.

When he finished, he turned to us.

"Your turn, young ladies."

When we began, I forgot Randall and floated into the variation. Soon my summer wind lifted me and carried me to the final pose.

Randall pounded his stick almost on my toes.

"Please notice, Madame Ballerina, everyone ended the variation as demonstrated except you."

Looking at the other girls, I saw that they were in a different pose, neither the one we learned in Martina's class, nor the one I learned last Christmas.

Randall wagged his stick at me.

"They danced it as I demonstrated. You, Madame Ballerina, performed it your way. Or else you didn't pay attention! Which was it?"

I couldn't answer. I stared at the floor.

"Did you pay attention?" Randall shouted.

"No, sir, I'm sorry."

He banged his stick.

"Dismissed!"

I ran from the classroom without looking at anybody. Especially not at Martina.

Monday afternoon, when I arrived at the ballet school, I didn't bother to look at the call board. I went straight to the dressing room, where Kathy was pulling on her tights.

"Did you see your name?" she asked.

"I didn't even look. What's the use?"

"Well, it's there, Maggie."

I couldn't believe her! I ran out to the board. There it was, first on the alphabetical list: Adams, Maggie. I found Kathy's too.

Opposite her name were the words: *Act I, party guest; Act II, corps, Waltz of Flowers.* The first was only a walk-on part, but the second was an excellent dancing role. Excellent for a student, anyway.

Opposite my name were the words: *Act I, party guest; Act II, angel.* Two walk-ons. No dancing at all.

My sudden excitement collapsed. I tried not to cry. When I turned away, I almost bumped into Martina. She put an arm around me.

"Never mind, Maggie. The important thing is that you learned something!"

Chapter Twenty-Five

A few weeks later I learned another important lesson, this time from Doug.

One noon, when I came out of Spanish class, he was standing in the hall. His curly blond head rested against the green stucco wall. His lanky frame sloped from wide shoulders to narrow waist to lean, long-muscled legs. Opening in a deep v at the throat, his white shirt disappeared into jeans the color of his hair. He twisted his hands behind him.

"Hi, Mag, I've been waiting to talk to you."

I glanced back at the classroom clock. It seemed to watch me like a big round eye. I shook my hair away from my face.

"I've got to run, Doug, to catch my bus."

"That's what I want to talk about, Mag. I've told you I really like you. And I think you like me, too. Right?"

I nodded.

"So, since we both like each other," he continued, "could we try to plan time to be together?"

He peered down at me. At the center of his blue eyes, golden flecks gleamed. I looked away.

"I'd like to, but with ballet..."

He interrupted.

"Don't say no, Mag. Think. There must be a few hours a week when you're not dancing or rehearsing. We could plan to be together then. Isn't there any time?"

I thought.

"Well, maybe on Sundays."

He took my hand.

"You see? How about this Sunday?'

"Well, Sunday night we're going to my uncle's."

"Can't you get out of it?"

I shook my head.

"It's a party for my father's forty-second birthday. He wants time with me too, you know. But what about Sunday afternoon? I could manage that. We could go on a picnic or something."

He swung my hand.

"I knew you could work it out, if you tried."

He laughed, showing his beautiful even teeth. If only mine were as beautiful!

Running to catch my bus, I vowed to ask Mama to phone my orthodontist. Then, remembering she went to college now, I vowed to call him myself.

Next morning I phoned him, and on Thursday I saw him.

"Still want those braces off, Maggie?" he asked as soon as I settled in his chair. He didn't even wait for an answer.

"Okey-dokey. 'The time has come, the walrus said.' And what a gorgeous bite you have now, my child, not to mention zee smile. But you'll still have to wear a retainer at night."

So, when Doug picked me up early Sunday afternoon, I greeted him with a huge smile, teeth together, lips curled back.

"Look! No braces."

"Terrific, Mag!" He put my picnic contribution of French bread and cheese into the trunk of the car. "But, to tell the truth, I never noticed your braces."

Driving into the foothills, we stopped beside a small blue lake and picnicked on the grass. After lunch, we stretched out under a birch tree to watch two sailboats heel before the wind. Above us, birch leaves colored and shaped like coins clicked and whirred, spun and shivered. In the filtered shade, I shivered too. Doug put an arm around me.

"Winter's coming," he said. "And Christmas."

I nodded, laughing.

"And the *Nutcracker*."

"It comes with the season, doesn't it?" he said. "Like Santa Claus and Christmas carols. But I don't care, if now and then you'll save me an hour of your time."

He leaned down and kissed me. His mouth felt soft and gentle.

For a little while that autumn afternoon I forgot about the *Nutcracker*, but not again until long after Christmas. Every day there were rehearsals: studio rehearsals, theatre rehearsals, rehearsals with and without orchestra, technical rehearsals, and dress rehearsals. Then the performances began.

Besides dancing in the city, the company performed out of town, including twice in our civic theatre, where our regional company danced last Christmas. Following the evening performance

159

there, I found Joyce waiting in the old basement dressing room we shared a year ago with Lupe.

Joyce patted the angel wig of pale spun glass that billowed around my head.

"Looks like Mrs. Bellermont's hairdo, Mag."

She hugged me, laughing.

"How are you doing, kid?"

I smiled.

"Good. How about you?"

"Mag, I love the university. Art history and Western civ are terrific—they're helping me tie all my scattered ideas together—helping me see the big picture. I like Greek, too, but it's a lot of work."

While I creamed off my makeup and changed, we traded gossip.

"Tell me about fat old Cyn," Joyce said.

"She's not so fat anymore. She stopped eating so much when she stopped dancing. You did know that she quit the company and quit dancing, didn't you?"

"No!"

"Yes! And the company's sort of fallen apart. When Cynthia quit, her mother quit the Auxiliary. I didn't believe McMichael when he said the company depended on Mrs. B. But he was right!"

"So that's why he's not putting on *Nutcracker* this year."

I nodded.

"But after Christmas he plans to hold auditions, Libbie says, and put on a spring season. I thought I wrote you."

"Mag, you never wrote once."

I shrugged and hung my head.

"I've been busy."

Her gray eyes regarded me.

"Too busy even to visit Lupe, she tells me."

160

I sighed.

"I know. I feel terrible about it. But I hate to see her just lying around, watching TV. Besides I'm always taking classes or rehearsing or something. I guess you saw her though."

"Yes, this afternoon. I tried to persuade her to come with me tonight, but she wouldn't."

"How is she?"

"Fatter. But—I know what you mean about her. Somehow, her sparkle's gone."

I nodded.

"She hasn't started dancing again. But my father says maybe she will after a while. She still goes to therapy."

Joyce asked about Libbie, but a knock interrupted my answer.

"Miss Adams, you're wanted in the director's office. Immediately."

I jumped up.

"Oh, Lord! What have I done now?"

I gave a quick brush at my hair.

Joyce laughed.

"They probably just want you to dance Sugarplum at tomorrow's matinee. That's all. Remember the hassle last year?"

I groaned.

"Don't remind me!"

Before I dashed out, we made a date to have lunch together before Joyce returned to college.

Upstairs, the director answered my tap with a booming: "Come in!"

In his office huddled Linda Larson, thin and pale and weeping. Without makeup, her face looked molded out of snow. With one hand she clutched together the lapels of her gray cloth coat.

"You can't expect me to do it," she cried. "With tonight and the matinee tomorrow, I'm exhausted. Totally."

The director motioned me to sit down and patted Linda's shoulder. She sobbed into a damp rag of a handkerchief.

"And I simply can't do that thing tomorrow morning. I won't. I'll resign first."

The director smoothed his mustache and tried to soothe Linda.

"Now, Linda, calm yourself. That's why we called in this young lady—what's your name again?"

"Maggie Adams."

He nodded.

"Yes. Well, according to Martina, Maggie knows the variation and performs it exceptionally well."

Both turned to me. Linda's eyes still spilled tears. The director cleared his throat.

"Tomorrow morning we want you to dance at an elementary school, a sort of publicity-community service thing. You're to do the Sugarplum variation."

I gasped with excitement. Joyce thought she was kidding, but they did want me to dance Sugarplum. Although—of course—not exactly in a regular performance!

The director raised his eyebrows.

"You don't mind, then? Good. You won't have to go out alone. There'll be a company member with you to show slides and tell the school children about the *Nutcracker.*"

Chapter Twenty=Six

The next morning I needed a ride to the demonstration. But Mama couldn't drive me, because she had an eight o'clock class. And my father would be leaving in a few minutes to see hospital patients.

Outside, rain drops crawled down the breakfast room windows. I stared at the storm and shivered in my bathrobe. Across the table my father sat behind the wall of his newspaper. Mama got up and set her dishes in the sink.

"Why don't you call Joyce?" Mama asked. "I'm sure she would be happy to drive you."

I watched Mama put on her raincoat and pick up her notebook and stack of textbooks. She sure took college seriously! And she had taken to wearing her hair swinging loose around her shoulders in a fragrant, coppery mass.

"I suppose I could call Joyce," I said, sighing.

Sometimes I almost wished Mama hadn't decided to live her own life.

After her car slid past the breakfast room windows, my father lowered his newspaper wall.

"Need a ride, do you, Maggie?"

I nodded and repeated the reason.

He set down his paper.

"I'm not deaf, you know. I heard you telling your mother about the demonstration. Can you wait till I'm through at the hospital? I had planned to take the rest of the morning off to play tennis with Chuck. But look at the rain!"

Two hours later, we found the school after winding through suburban streets that were too new to be on the map. My father parked near a group of green stucco cubes called Marsh Creek Elementary School.

"Rabbit hutch modern," my father labeled the buildings. "What ever happened to the handsome weathered brick schools of my day?"

I didn't answer. My head was too busy remembering the steps of the Sugarplum variation.

With my ballet bag dangling from my shoulder, I walked along the wet walk beside my father. It was no longer raining, but a cold wind rushed between the green buildings. I was glad I had decided to wear my thick blue sweater. I noticed that over his white shirt, my father wore his sweater that matched mine. Mama knit both of them before she started to college. With our matching sweaters and red hair nobody could doubt that we were father and daughter!

The spaces between the buildings buzzed with children's voices, and through the windows we saw students working at tables. Soon we found a large rectangular cube labeled Multipurpose Room.

"This must be it," I said.

I shoved open one of the double doors. Inside, shouting instructions to a janitor, paced Larry Randall.

Oh, no, I thought. He always turned up to spoil my life!

He eyed me and turned his long, narrow back on me.

"That's the dressing room," he said, as if still speaking to the janitor, "behind that red door."

His words hummed through his nose and he showed no further interest in me.

I remained at the front door with my father.

"I—I didn't know you'd be here, Mr. Randall," I stammered. I was ashamed that he ignored me like this when my father was here.

Randall swung around. His nostrils flared.

"I didn't ask to come. I'm not here by choice."

He flung his words into the big empty room.

"This community service nonsense is a waste of an artist's time and talents," he added, motioning the janitor to move the table an inch to the left.

My father pulled the door closed behind us. His words came out like cold separate ice cubes.

"My daughter has been requested to perform here this morning. I would appreciate your helping her as much as possible."

Randall arched his eyebrows. It was easy to see that he didn't care for my father's commanding tone.

"I'm not here to babysit," he said. "She's on her own. And it'll be a miracle if she can stay on her feet in this slippery barn of a place!"

He waved his hand at the huge, plain room. I had to agree that it was more like a vacant barn than a theatre. Except for the big round clock, the green walls stretched bare. Linoleum squares paved the concrete floor. Folding metal chairs waited in stiff rows. Then I noticed the worst thing of all—except maybe the hard, unyielding concrete floor.

"There's no stage!" I cried.

Randall sneered.

"So? Get dressed."

"But where will I dance?"

He pointed a thin, long finger.

"There. Up front. Where they've left you a strip of bare linoleum. Slippery as glass. I'm afraid this isn't Lincoln Center, young lady, but then you're not Makarova, either So get dressed."

My face burned and I noticed that my father's face turned bright red, too. His hands tightened into fists. I laid a hand on his arm to try to keep him from saying something awful. I felt how tense his muscles were.

"It's all right, Father," I whispered. "He's always like this. You can go now. I'll get a ride home somehow."

My father frowned.

"I don't care for his attitude."

I laughed a little.

"I don't much either. But I'll be okay. And thanks for driving me."

"Don't mention it. Maybe I should have done it before. It gave us a chance to be together, didn't it?"

After my father went out, I pushed open the red door into the so-called "dressing room."

It wasn't any more a dressing room than the Multipurpose Room was a theatre. There wasn't even a mirror, but, fortunately, I had fixed my hair at home and put on a little eye shadow. In the room, the school kept a refrigerator and a few folding chairs. I

166

shivered. The room was as cold as the inside of that refrigerator.

On a wire hanger, hooked to the handle of the refrigerator, dangled a limp pink costume. It reminded me of cotton candy that some child has carried around so long that it's turning back to syrup. But I had worn worse costumes.

Pulling on my tights and toe shoes, I looked for water. I needed some to wet the heels of my satin shoes so that they wouldn't come off or slip on the linoleum. Finally, I rubbed on some frost I found in the freezer compartment.

Randall poked his yellow head into the room.

"The children are coming in. Aren't you in your costume yet?"

"I haven't warmed up."

"Warmed up! Good lord, you're not dancing for Walter Terry! Just a couple of hundred brats. They just want to see a pretty costume. You don't have to warm up to mark."

My cheeks grew hot.

"I never mark! I'd be ashamed to mark."

I didn't add "like you did last Christmas!" But Randall seemed to get the point. He slammed out of the dressing room and I started *pliés*.

Through the closed door, I heard children settling on the metal chairs. I also heard Randall's affected voice describing the *Nutcracker*.

When my muscles felt limber, I pulled on the pink costume. The bodice sagged and the tutu drooped against my thighs. I longed for Ida and her pincushion bracelet, but I used safety pins to tuck in the waist. Unlike last year, I didn't need tissues to fill out the little darted cups in the bodice.

167

I was fluffing out the layers of pink net when Randall butted in again.

"Get out here," he said. "I've finished the slides and they're waiting for you."

My old fear returned for a minute. I pushed at my hair where it seemed to be frizzing out of the net. Did I remember the steps? But of course, I did, I told myself. And I no longer wore braces! At last, I was a dancer! I crossed my fingers, pulled in my waist, and stepped through the doorway.

"And here, dear children," Randall said, "is the young lady who will dance the Sugarplum Fairy variation this morning."

Smiling at the children, I stepped onto the slippery linoleum.

In the front rows huddled the youngest. They sat cross-legged on the bare linoleum. Their knees and scuffed shoes framed the narrow space left for me to dance. Behind them, older children made the metal chairs squeak. Way at the back, where some of the teachers sat, loomed my father. His red hair and blue sweater clashed with the green stucco wall.

I was so surprised that he was still there, that for a moment I lost my poise. I stared. He smiled and wagged his fingers at me in a funny little salute. With him there, I felt even more nervous, but I took my first pose and waited for Randall to start the tape. I heard the children whispering. At my feet a little girl sighed.

"She looks exactly like the Sugarplum Fairy should!" she said.

Thick glasses magnified her brown eyes.

"Oh, yes!" Her friends agreed.

When the music tinkled from the tape recorder, the children hushed.

At first, my *arabesques* skated forward on the slick linoleum, but I leaned into them and did not fall. My *pirouettes* skidded sideways, but I managed to land safely. My *glissades* slid almost into the frame of knees. But, looking down, I saw how wide the little girl's brown eyes had grown behind her glasses. I felt my summer wind begin to stir.

I smiled. I almost laughed. I was a bird lifted on warm currents, carried above the tawny coastal hills. Soon I became the wind itself—my gentle, whispering, summer wind.

Suddenly, I heard snickers. Had these children noticed my feet slipping on the linoleum? In a moment, however, I saw that they were not laughing at me. They were laughing at brown-eyed Clara. In her scuffed shoes and short plaid skirt, she danced beside me.

"Sit down, stupid," some of the children hissed.

But I took her hand. We danced the rest of the variation together, Clara and I.

When the music ended, a teacher snatched her back to the floor. I looked at the eyes behind the thick glasses. Had her dance ended too suddenly? Would she cry? But her huge eyes spun with happiness. Clara must have been feeling a summer wind of her own.

When the clapping ended, and the teachers herded away the children, Randall arched a thin eyebrow at me.

"Under the circumstances, young lady, you could have done worse. Not that I'm predicting you'll become a dancer, mind you."

I glanced at him. Was he complimenting me? For some reason I remembered Joyce's ballet. I felt as if I had won the Golden Shoes.

"Thank you," I said.

Shrugging, he bent over the recorder.

"Don't thank me, although I have seen worse beginning dancers."

Breathless, I rushed back to my father.

"Randall actually complimented me! Almost, anyway. That's a miracle!"

My father smiled. He nodded thoughtfully.

"And I saw why you want to be a dancer. It showed, Maggie, how much you love dancing."

He laid an arm around my shoulders that were still wet with sweat.

"You must feel like I feel when my backhand return perfectly skims the net. It's no longer me stroking the tennis ball. Some magic takes over."

I nodded up at him. I grabbed his hand.

"Oh, thanks for staying, Father. And for understanding."

I was too shy to suggest that his magic and my summer wind were the same thing.

He laughed.

"My pleasure. But don't think I'm forgetting to be practical. I still want you to learn typing and shorthand. And try to save a little time to be with us, Maggie."

He squeezed my shoulders.

"By the way, someone's trying to attract your attention."

I turned around and saw some children rushing toward me. In the lead came brown-eyed Clara. She pushed a scrap of paper and a pencil into my hands. She waited. Her eyes spun behind her thick glasses. Beside me my father laughed.

"Well, sign it, Maggie. She wants your autograph."

I giggled.

"I've never done this before. What'll I write?"

But the words came to me as naturally as my summer wind.

"Love to Clara," I wrote and signed my name.

Maggie Adams, Dancer.

THE REAL ME
by Betty Miles

"My book is not the kind that tells 'How Tomboy Mindy discovered that growing up gracefully can be as fun as playing baseball.'

"I have often thought how relaxing it would be to be invisible. But when I took over Richard's paper route they said 'girls can't deliver papers.' And when I wanted to take tennis instead of slimnastics, they said 'girls like to do graceful feminine things.' So I had to speak out. I only wanted things to be fair.

"My book is for anyone who might want to read about the life and thoughts of a person like me. If some boy wants to read this, go ahead. Maybe you will learn something."

An Avon Camelot Book
48199 $1.50

An action-packed baseball story!

MY FATHER, THE COACH

by Alfred Slote

Ezell Corkins had good news and bad news for the Sumpter
Street gang. The good news was that they were to become the
Atlas Movers . . . a *real* Little League team. The bad news
was that his father, Willie Corkins, would be the coach.

An embarrassed Ezell is caught between fellow teammates
and a father who seems less interested in baseball than in
beating the rival coach. Just what is a fellow supposed to do?

An Avon Camelot Book
49809 $1.50

"Harold waited to see if he could catch sight of that glint of steel he was always hearing about. The gun barrel. He thought of how he must look standing there, fat and pale and scared. The perfect target . . ."

AFTER THE GOAT MAN

by Betsy Byars

illustrated by Ronald Himler

When Harold played Monopoly with Ada and Figgy, he always won. He could make his voice sound deep and important on the phone. And he had a WCLG Golden Oldie T-shirt. But nothing could make up for the fact that he was fat. Harold thought he was the most miserable person in the world, until the night that Figgy's eccentric grandfather picked up a shotgun and disappeared.

Then, when Figgy was badly injured in an accident, it was suddenly up to Harold to find the Goat Man. And on the way, he discovered that his problems were very small compared with the problems of other people.

An Avon Camelot Book
41590 $1.95

Also by Betsy Byars
RAMA THE GYPSY CAT   41608 $1.25
THE WINGED COLT OF CASA MIA   46995 $1.50

Avon Camelot Books are available at your bookstore. Or, you may use Avon's special mail order service. Please state the title and code number and send with your check or money order for the full price, plus 50¢ per copy to cover postage and handling, to: AVON BOOKS, Mail Order Department, 224 West 57th Street, New York· New York 10019. Please allow 4-6 weeks for delivery.

An old mansion, a graveyard, and a mysterious skull!

UNCLE ROBERT'S SECRET

by Wylly Folk St. John

"You don't know what scared is till you've fallen out of a tree late at night into a bunch of broken-down gravestones, practically on top of somebody you think might be a mean guy . . . and there's an awful scream still ringing in your ears."

Bob should have known how hard it would be to keep a secret, especially when that secret happened to be a bedraggled little boy named Tim. And when Bob finally shared it with his brother and sister, they suddenly found themselves involved in a very spooky mystery.

An Avon Camelot Book
46326 $1.50

Gilly Ground was an orphan and all he wanted was a little peace and quiet . . .

DORP DEAD

by Julia Cunningham

illustrated by James Spanfeller

Life in the orphanage was difficult in many ways. Gilly spent as much time as he could in the abandoned tower in the woods. It was peaceful there—and it was there that Gilly met the Hunter. Then, one day, he was placed in a foster home. And Gilly felt as though he were trapped in a nightmare come true.

An Avon Camelot Book
51458 $1.95

Also by Julia Cunningham
DEAR RAT   46615 $1.50

Avon Camelot Books are available at your bookstore. Or, you may use Avon's special mail order service. Please state the title and code number and send with your check or money order for the full price, plus 50¢ per copy to cover postage and handling, to: AVON BOOKS, Mail Order Department, 224 West 57th Street New York, New York 10019. Please allow 4-6 weeks for delivery.

A suspenseful mystery with a surprise ending!

THE CHRISTMAS TREE MYSTERY

by Wylly Folk St. John

Beth Carlton was in trouble. She accused Pete Abel of steal-
ing the Christmas ornaments from her family tree, something
she knew he hadn't done. And what was worse—the police
believed her! Beth had two days to prove to the police that
Pete wasn't a thief, and all she had to go on was her step-
brother's word that Pete was innocent.

An Avon Camelot Book
46300 $1.50